Dedication
Acknowledgements

Table of Contents

Treachery
Climate of Fire Book Two

Shirley Bigelow DeKelver

Print ISBNs
Amazon print 9780228633136
Ingram Spark 9780228633143
Barnes & Noble 9780228633150
BWL Print 9780228633167

BWL Publishing Inc.

Books we love to write ...
Authors around the world.

http://bwlpublishing.ca

Chapter 1

We reached the top of the summit. I walked over and stood at the edge of the precipice. I stared moodily at the churning river far below, captivated by the brilliant hues of the autumn leaves. I wrapped my arms tightly around my waist and shivered. A few late blooming wildflowers and herbs grew sparsely in the surrounding meadow. In the distance I spotted smoke rising from the dense forest.

"Wildfire," Taylor announced, as he stopped next to me. "I imagine they will burn well into November."

I shrugged, saying nothing. My thoughts returned to the meadow. Taylor allowed me a day to grieve, and dreading the imminent arrival of winter and the Desert Rats, decided it was time to move on. Everyone pitched in folding the tents and packing the supplies. I reached for Rusty's backpack and shook out its contents, it contained his clothing, a few shiny rocks, and two crumpled comics. I froze, finding it difficult to breathe. Taylor, who had been watching, reached down, and picked up the clothes.

"Here, put these in your backpack, the kids can always use additional garments."

I nodded and did as he asked. Eddie had approached me and quietly asked if he could have his brother's rocks and comics, and I handed them to him.

We left the meadow heading eastward, covering as many kilometres as possible. We were a solemn group, our thoughts elsewhere, each of us accepting the reasons for our haste. The first night we set up camp, Eddie had run away, intent on returning to the meadow. Taylor backtracked and found him, realizing he was struggling with his brother's death, and needed time to accept he was gone.

The paths were steep, and the air turned colder. The bitterly freezing wind made our lives miserable. I listened to Debbie's raspy wheezing as we climbed and Mai-Li suggested she and Eddie breathe through their noses instead of their mouths. She was troubled about Debbie's respiratory problems. Eddie had lost weight, and I worried about him as well.

My thoughts returned to the present; I looked one last time at the view. Taylor retrieved his packs and weapons, his signal for us to resume our journey. I moved back from the ledge and took my place in line behind Mai-Li and Debbie.

That night we set up camp in a sheltered burrow, the next night in a shaft in an abandoned mine. Taylor and Willie hunted in the evenings while Mai-Li and I set up camp; at times, the guys were lucky, sometimes they returned empty-handed. The deer meat provided by the firestorm was a blessing, however our food supply rapidly disappeared. Mai-Li never passed a bush or a plant without stopping to see if she could use the berries or herbs, her knowledge of edible and medicinal plants proved invaluable. She was so excited when we passed a bilberry bush (to me a cheap imitation of blueberries) or bear berries, as she called them. Everyone pitched in and picked. She brewed tea or mixed them in the deer stew to add flavour, or dried them to be used as medicines. Nothing was wasted.

Each night, graphic nightmares of Rusty's death returned, and I would lie awake for hours, replaying it over and over in my mind. My bitterness festered like a septic wound. I blamed myself for suggesting we turn north and head to the Wastelands, unaware of the risks that lay ahead. I often spotted Taylor watching me, and I would look away. I was exhausted all the time and my lack of appetite worried him. Losing one of our own was catastrophic, and each of us struggled with depression and anger in his own way.

Foraging for food proved to be a time-consuming process, and surprisingly Taylor never complained as we slowed our pace. Perhaps, he accepted the fact we would not reach our destination before winter arrived;

and that our main priority now was to replenish our dwindling food supply.

The nights turned bitter and the game became scarcer. At times Taylor often backtracked, handing Rusty's compass to Willie, instructing him to stay on course. He never mentioned it to us, but I knew he was concerned about being followed by the Desert Rats. Their leader, Lars, was ruthless and unforgiving, and when Taylor had discovered their stockpile of guns and seized a few of their rifles and ammunition in retaliation for attacking us, it did not sit well with Lars.

We plodded through heavy undergrowth and discovered animal trails and meandering streams which provided much-needed water. The first time I tried to bath Squishy, a battle erupted. Eddie and Debbie refused to hand him over; their logic being Squishy would catch a cold if I plunged him into the icy water. I shrugged and wandered back to help Mai-Li with supper, accepting defeat. The least of our problems was a smelly, battered teddy bear.

Late one afternoon, after stopping earlier than usual, Taylor suggested we look for an underground shelter. I knew he was troubled about being in the open if it snowed, and in the event the Desert Rats caught up with us.

"Debbie, remember to look for an animal house, okay?"

Debbie grinned and waved at Taylor. Generally, she was content, although at times she seemed aware of everybody's pain in losing Rusty. She didn't throw her ball as often, she held it rigidly in her hand, never letting it go, when she ate and when she slept.

Mai-Li and I were often overwhelmed watching two young children and cooking and cleaning for six people. Debbie needed continuous care, and Eddie never spoke or laughed anymore. He mourned the loss of his brother, and he responded only to Taylor. I ached inside, missing his peaceful demeanor and insightful chatter. If I tried talking to him, he never answered. There was no laughter, no singing; the joy was gone, and watching Eddie interact with Taylor broke my heart.

Two days later, we stopped earlier than usual when Debbie pointed towards a cave opening. Taylor motioned for us to lie flat on the ground. He soon returned, announcing it was an underground den, and would be perfect for the night. We laid the tarp on the cave floor and set up the small tent as there was not enough room to install the larger one. We piled our packs and provisions in the far corner. Mai-Li started a fire near the entrance and we ate left-over deer stew with crackers. We doused the flames; aware a campfire could be seen for miles and inform the Desert Rats of our location. A full moon shone that night, which provided ample light to manoeuvre in the cave. We used Taylor's flashlight only when necessary, if the batteries died, we would be down to one, which Mai-Li carried and used only for emergencies.

"This is perfect, Debbie," I replied enthusiastically, praising the young girl. "You must be magic; you always find animal houses."

"Yes, I am magic. Why does it smell in here?"

"It's an underground den, and an animal probably lives here."

"Is he goanna come home and chase us away?"

"Don't worry, Taylor and Willie will watch out for him, we'll be safe."

Taylor and Willie returned from inspecting the area around the den and overheard our conversation. "It's a bear den, Debbie," Taylor revealed. "He's getting ready to hibernate."

"Hibernate means he's going to nap a long time, that's what Eddie told me," Debbie added.

"That's true, bears sleep in the winter, they don't wake up until spring, when it gets warmer."

Debbie nodded sagely, then turned her attention back to her ball.

Taylor smiled and ruffled Eddie's hair when he joined him at the cave entrance.

"Did you guys discover anything?" Mai-Li questioned.

Taylor leaned his rifle against the inside wall of the cave and shook his head. Willie wandered to the back of the den and laid his weapon on the ground next to his gear.

"Is it safe to stay here for the night?" I asked. "What if the bear returns?"

"He's in the area," Taylor announced, turning to face me. "We found his tracks; he's not far from here. It's probably wise to go on guard tonight. Mai-Li and I will take the first shift, then you and Willie can take the second."

I wondered why Taylor paired me with Willie. Did he blame me for suggesting we detour through the Wastelands, ultimately putting us in danger, not only from the firestorm but, from the Desert Rats as well?

I raised my head. Taylor, Mai-Li, and Willie were watching me, waiting for my answer.

"Yeah, that's fine," I answered half-heartedly.

"Great," Taylor replied, as he turned and faced Mai-Li. "The sooner the kids settle for the night, the earlier we can leave in the morning."

Our long hike had exhausted them, and it did not take long for them to fall asleep. Taylor turned to Mai-Li, "You ready?"

She nodded, then pointed at her cane tied around her waist.

"You're positive you don't want my gun or maybe Carlie's rifle, I'm not convinced your cane is weapon enough if we meet up with the bear. From the size of his tracks, he's a big one?"

Mai-Li raised her head regally. "It is not the cane that wields the power, it is the person using it."

At first Taylor did not respond; he studied Mai-Li's face for the longest time. Then he smiled, and said, "I'm quite aware of your proficiency, Mai-Li, but a hibernating bear is mean, angry, and hungry."

My mind was racing, what just happened? Did Taylor have feelings for Mai-Li? Why should that upset me, I had made it obvious many times, I was not interested in him or his advances.

Fully clothed, I crawled inside my bedroll, which was between Taylor and Willy's sleeping bags. I tossed and turned, and eventually fell into a restless sleep.

Chapter Two

Someone was shaking my shoulder; I opened my eyes to darkness. "It's me," Mai-Li whispered. "Shift change, did the kids wake up?"

"No," I whispered. "They haven't stirred."

Mai-Li crawled into the small tent where Debbie and Eddie were sleeping. "Goodnight Carlie, stay alert."

I rose and stumbled in the direction of my backpack. I bumped against somebody. "Sorry," I murmured.

Hands grabbed my shoulders and steadied me. It was Taylor. "Wouldn't it be great if Willie woke as easily as you."

"I'm a light sleeper," I mumbled, groaning inwardly. *Great comeback, Carlie.*

I heard a click as Taylor turned on his flashlight, I knelt and rummaged through my bag, and removed my warm sweater and scarf. I sat on the ground, and pulled on my boots, making sure my knife was safely tucked inside its sheath.

I lifted my head; Taylor watched me sharply. "It worries me you only have a knife for protection. It's okay for smaller animals but not if you stumble across a cougar or a bear. As soon as we have an opportunity, I'm going to give you shooting lessons, it's time you learned how to manage a rifle."

"I don't believe it's a big cat or a bear worrying you. I notice you glance behind us all the time; you're uneasy about the Desert Rats."

Taylor shrugged, then looked away, staring into the darkness. Something else was bothering him, and all at once, I realized what it was.

"You're concerned about more than Lars, aren't you? It's me, isn't it? I know I've not contributed as much as the others, and increasingly I'm beginning to understand it wasn't my fault Rusty died." I rambled. "It's just that the pain is so intense at times."

Taylor frowned, then ran his fingers through his hair.

"What, what.... are you talking about? Why do you think it was your fault?"

"The shooter aimed his gun at me; I was his target. He fired the same time I threw my knife and he shot Rusty instead."

Taylor knelt to my level, gazed directly at me, and sighed. "I guess that explains a lot."

I played with my boot laces, unable to look at him. "Mai-Li told me you stayed near me after we left the train car, you were the only one who could control me."

"You woke up crying and screaming, you scared the kids, and the rest of us worried you might not recover."

"Taylor, I'm sorry I was so much trouble, but I don't remember leaving the train car or walking for days across the Wastelands. I don't remember any of it."

The tears streamed down my face, and I wiped them away with the back of my hand. I was annoyed with myself, I always loathed crying, especially in front of others, and lately, it seemed as if I couldn't stop.

"Carlie, your memory will return, but right now you need to look forward."

"I know, I'm trying."

Taylor pulled me close and held me, then he leaned over and whispered. "When we set up camp tomorrow, I'm going to start your training. Willie can give Mai-Li a hand with supper."

He must have realized what he said when suddenly both of us started to giggle. Mai-Li popped her head out of the tent and hushed us sternly. The unwritten rule was anyone who woke Debbie had to stay awake until she fell back to sleep, which was not always easy to do.

It took at least ten minutes to get Willie moving, he shuffled around the den, then dug through his bag for his warmer clothes. As we turned to leave, Taylor tapped his shoulder. "You should probably take your rifle, Willie."

Willie shrugged, returned to his bedroll, and retrieved his weapon. I was not too pleased being partnered with him as his hunting prowess left little to be desired, although I had to admit his behaviour towards me had improved considerably since we left the Wastelands.

We edged slowly out of the den, Taylor followed and turned his flashlight in a circular motion, searching for signs of the bear. Satisfied we were alone, he pointed towards an animal trail leading upwards to a rocky embankment. "Stay on the path, don't wander off or you'll get lost; I don't want to search for you in the middle of the night, remember to stay focused at all times."

Taylor handed his flashlight to Willie. We walked towards the trail, it was too dark to see the surrounding area, although we did have a shadowy view of the cave opening. I scurried to catch up with him, we climbed for a brief period, then I pulled his sleeve to catch his attention.

"Let's not go any higher, if we spot the bear, we need time to return to the cave to warn the others," I suggested.

Willie nodded and sat down on a flat rock. The moon appeared from behind a cloud. It cast a reflection on the surrounding foliage and he clicked off the flashlight. An owl hooted, and crickets chirped. Neither of us started a conversation, I was content to sit quietly. Hours passed, Willie settled back and fell asleep, dead to the world.

I rested my chin on my raised knees, the moon disappeared, and it was so dark, I couldn't see my hands in front of my face. It was then I heard a guttural cough coming from the bushes. I reached over and shook Willie, who grabbed his rifle as he sat up in alarm.

"What?"

"Quiet," I whispered. "I just heard something."

"Where?"

"Below us, in the bushes."

"What should we do?"

I turned to look at Willie, it was a lucky thing for him it was so dark he couldn't see my face. I was unarmed except for my knife, and my back-up, who carried a loaded rifle, asked "What do we DO?"

"Maybe we should look and see what made the noise?" I answered, straining to keep the sarcasm from my voice.

"Did it sound like a bear?"

"I don't know, it could be anything, but we can't stay here all night."

"Okay, let's go. I'll be right behind you."

I lowered my head, biting my tongue. "I have a better proposal. Since you're the one carrying a rifle, how about you go first."

Willie grunted and handed me the flashlight. He cautiously stepped in front of me. The moon appeared as the clouds dispersed. I trailed him down the incline; we heard movement in the shrubbery below us, then a muffled growl.

"Shit," Willie hissed. "Sounds like a bear to me."

"There," I alerted as I pointed towards the cave. The dark outline of a huge animal shuffled towards the opening, swaying its head back and forth, raking its claws in the dirt. I detected a movement beside me, I turned and looked at Willie. "Let's not turn on the flashlight," I whispered. "We don't want him to know we're here, he could just as easily come after us. It knows something's in the cave; we must warn the others."

We inched noiselessly down the hill, sidestepping and avoiding the dirt and rocks. Suddenly a shot shattered the stillness. We threw ourselves on the ground, a second shot followed. Willie cocked his rifle and I reached down and grabbed my knife. We cautiously got to our feet and crept quietly towards the cave. A dark silhouette moved in the shadows, and Taylor stepped into the open. He was standing over the carcass of a huge grizzly. I turned on the flashlight and aimed it in his direction. He nodded, reacting to our presence. I heard shuffling and spotted Mai-Li and the kids squatting inside the cave entrance.

"We heard a noise in the underbrush," I exclaimed, turning to face Taylor. "We didn't spot the bear until it was too late. We hurried as fast as we could to warn you, then we heard your gunshots, and hit the dirt."

"I believe he's been watching us since we got here," Taylor replied.

"How did you know he was outside the cave?"

"I found its tracks earlier and realized he was in the area. It was only a matter of time before he returned to his den. I couldn't relax, so I hid close to the access. He must have sensed my presence and waited until I revealed myself, then he charged, it took two shots for me to slay him."

Willie was circling the bear, as wound-up as a kid in a candy shop. "Wow, he's humungous, what are we going to do with him?"

"Winter is just around the corner," Taylor reminded. "We'll use his fur as a blanket, and we can smoke the meat. This bear is a gift and we can't leave it here for the scavengers. If we are careful, the meat should last until we find ourselves a place for the winter."

Mai-Li rose, holding Eddie and Debbie close. She turned and faced the rest of us. "We must show our gratitude to this magnificent creature by honouring its spirit."

Taylor placed his hand on Mai-Li's shoulder and nodded in agreement. He waited until Willie and I entered the den. "Get some sleep," he spoke. "Obviously, there's a change of plans, we won't be leaving tomorrow, we have a lot to do in the next couple of days."

"Let's hope the weather doesn't take a turn for the worse," Mai-Li added. "We still have a long trek in front of us and it's imperative we find shelter."

Chapter Three

The next morning, before Taylor and Mai-Li skinned the bear, Mai-Li asked everyone to sit in a circle around the campfire as she wanted to thank the animal's spirit by expressing our gratitude and seeking permission for taking its life. She said the bear was known for its courage which must be respected. It was a solemn ceremony, and I was pleased we honoured the magnificent creature.

Taylor skinned the carcass with his sharp knife and Mai-Li removed the meat and fat, I noticed nothing was wasted, she saved the heart and the liver as well. The hide was then stretched and placed flat on the ground to air dry. Then Mai-Li cut the fat into strips and Willie started a fire and helped her smoke the meat. Taylor kept his rifle close, as he was aware our fire would announce our location to the Desert Rats.

Mai-Li heated some of the bear fat in a pan and fried pieces of cracklings which she shared with all of us. It was delicious and the kids kept asking for more. I chuckled to myself as Debbie giggled and pointed at Eddie's face smeared with bear grease. Eddie casually wiped the back of his hand across his mouth, then nonchalantly wiped it across his jeans.

It didn't take the kids long to get bored, I decided to distract them by going on a hike, receiving strict orders from Taylor to stay within walking distance of the cave. We followed the trail Willie and I took the previous night when Eddie abruptly stopped and pointed to the ground. A frog was hiding in the rushes, he picked it up in the palm of his hand. I noticed how gentle he was, and I hoped his interest and curiosity about nature would aid him overcome his grief, even for a brief time. Debbie touched it with her finger, quickly pulling back.

"Yuck, he's all slimy," she exclaimed scrunching her face.

"That's because he lives in the water, most of the time," I laughed, "Frogs are important as they let us know how healthy the forests and the ponds are."

I noticed Eddie was listening to every word. He lowered his head, looked at the frog, and threw it into the undergrowth. I raced after it and was relieved to see it was not injured.

"Eddie, why did you do that?" I demanded sharply when I returned to where he was standing. "You might have hurt it?"

All I got was an indifferent shrug. Debbie laid her head on his shoulder, and Eddie reached over and took her hand.

"Do you two want to return to the cave?"

"Don't matter," Eddie replied.

"Alright, let's keep going, although if you find any more frogs you can't pick them up."

Again, he shrugged, I promised myself I would be more patient with him. It was so simple to forget others were hurting as well, especially Eddie, whose grief for the loss of his twin brother was deeper than the rest of us could fathom.

We continued our climb up the path and arrived at a field of withered wildflowers and dried grasses. I stopped and pointed to the ground.

"What is it?" Debbie asked, as she jumped back.

"It's a garter snake," Eddie replied. "There's lots of them in Vancouver, my dad used to say they were good guys cause they ate mice and voles."

"They ate them," Debbie exclaimed, staring in awe at Eddie.

Eddie nodded, then squatted and touched the snake. It was gone in a second.

"Do you like snakes, Eddie?" I probed.

He nodded, not raising his head. "My Mom wouldn't let Rusty or me bring them in the house. She was terrified of them, so we would sneak them into our bedroom and hide them in shoe boxes or tin cans. One day a snake got loose, and it snuck into the kitchen. Mom found it under the sink, she screamed so loud it hurt our ears. Rusty and I hid under our bed. We both got grounded for a whole week."

I stared at Eddie, then I started laughing and couldn't stop, tears rolled down my face. Soon both kids joined me, and we collapsed in a heap. I heard a shuffle in the bushes and Taylor dashed out, clutching his rifle. "What happened, are you guys alright?" he asked anxiously.

"Carlie found a snake," Debbie giggled.

"What's so funny about that?" Taylor answered sharply.

"Eddie's Mommy hated snakes, then Eddie's snake ran away and his Mommy found it in the kitchen. Eddie and Rusty got in big trouble."

Eddie, Debbie, and I laughed louder. Taylor shook his head in bewilderment, obviously relieved we were not in danger. Frowning irritably, he turned and pointed towards the cave. All three of us stood and headed down the trail.

"What happened?" Mai-Li questioned when we reached the cave. She grabbed the kids and held them tightly.

"They found a garter snake," Taylor declared, then returned to the bear carcass.

Mai-Li looked at me, and I wiped the tears from my face, grinning foolishly. Shaking her head, she ushered the kids inside. She gave them a drink of water and a cookie. Then she took out their crayons and paper and announced it was quiet time. Willie tagged along as he was never far away when cookies were handed out. He eyed the comics and the treat, noticed the look on Mai-Li's face, then turned and left.

I understood Taylor's frustration, as it was my responsibility to entertain the kids, yet laughing at Eddie's snake story relieved some of the uneasiness and tension I felt around him. In a small way, it opened a door, not only for me, but for him as well.

I squatted next to the fire, and remembered we would be here until the bear meat was smoked and dried. Trying to make amends, a brainstorm abruptly popped into my head.

"We must have a ton of dirty clothes, we haven't done laundry in ages," I mentioned. "There's a stream close by, if anyone wants something washed, bring them to me."

In five minutes, a pile of clothes reached as high as my knees. Taylor wrapped them in the tarp and handed it to me. "If you have time to do more, let me know." he grinned.

I scowled and entered the tent. I dug through our supplies and found the soap. A quarter of the box was left, Mai-Li and I always guarded it carefully.

"Carlie," Mai-Li suggested. "Let's not use the soap for now, we'll need it when it turns colder. You should be able to clean the clothes if you pound them against a rock."

I hesitated for a second, my mouth wide open. Then she took the box and put it back in the supply bag. Obviously, she was serious.

I picked up the tarp, threw it over my shoulder, and left. Grumbling under my breath, I realized it was Mai-Li's way of getting back at me when Taylor rushed to find out why the kids and I were making so much noise, thinking we were attacked by a bear or cougar. I know I startled them, but I did not feel any regret, it was exactly what Eddie and I needed.

I climbed the steep path, then headed towards the sound of running water. I found a flat area and untied the tarp. I scrubbed and bashed the soiled clothes against rocks, washing away soot and grime. My hands and fingers ached from the icy water. Then I draped the wet garments over the bushes to semi-dry. I would spread them on the cave floor tonight and let them dry some more, it would be a slow process as we would not have the campfire during the night.

I hummed while I worked, for the first time in ages I was content. I did not know what was ahead of us tomorrow or the day after. I realized I had not been providing enough support to the well-being of the group; I was a burden since leaving the Wastelands. It was time to pitch in and do my share.

However, if I could help it, laundry would not be high on my list of chores!

Chapter Four

It took two days for the bear to be skinned and smoked. We ate a quick breakfast, packed, and left at sunrise. We hiked for hours, and Taylor explained to Eddie how to use the compass by pointing it in the direction we were headed. We laboured through heavy underbrush, brambles and shrubs, our hands and faces scratched by the twigs and prickly leaves. Taylor was frustrated with our pace, often he looked back for signs of the Desert Rats, and I knew he was worried. Several times a day, he requested Willie to take the lead while he backtracked. They must be nearby, otherwise, Taylor would not have been as guarded.

Willie and Mai-Li both knew how to shoot, and in Taylor's case, as well as being an excellent shot he was proficient in archery. Mai-Li carried her cane and could defend herself with Kung-Fu, and over time I proved my skill with my knife. We each made a contribution in our own way and because of my inability to operate a gun, I understood Taylor's concern that I was the weakest link.

We stopped around noon for lunch, standing while we ate. Eddie and Debbie were quiet and sensed the tension in the group. Taylor motioned us to crouch, and we formed a tight circle, surrounded and hidden by shrubbery, even though I appreciated it offered false security.

"The Desert Rats are approximately two kilometres behind us," he whispered.

None of us spoke, and I realized it was time for me to get involved. I pointed to one of the stolen rifles Taylor was toting in his backpack.

He immediately understood what I wanted. He removed the weapon, opened a box of ammo, and loaded the magazine. Then he handed it to me. "The trigger guard is on and in the event you need to fire, release it. Keep your hand steady on the barrel, it will provide you with more accuracy."

I nodded, terrified, as I was aware he knew I'd never fired a weapon in my life. My hand shook, which I'm guessing wasn't reassuring. I didn't dare inform him I had no clue how to release the trigger guard.

He leaned over and whispered to Mai-Li. "Leave most of the supplies here, take Eddie and Debbie over to the thicket next to those trees. Look for a suitable hiding place and try to keep them quiet. Do not move until you spot us returning. If you hear gunshots, remain hidden. We may be gone for a while. Here, take my gun, we have the rifles."

Mai-Li nodded, took the weapon and a handful of bullets from Taylor, rose, grabbed the smaller bag holding water and food, put the gun and bullets inside, and tied it around her waist. She gripped the kids' hands. Eddie turned and looked directly at me, waved, then they disappeared in the undergrowth.

"Alright, shadow me," Taylor ordered. "Be as quiet as you can, they know where we are."

I looked at Taylor, and he smiled and nodded, as he must have sensed my anxiety and fear. I gulped and tightened my grip on the rifle.

"I'll go first," he whispered, "Carlie, next and Willie you take the rear."

We crept through the scrub. Taylor raised his hand signalling us to stop. I felt Willie's warm breath on my neck. I tolerated his closeness, realizing now was not the time to recommend he back off.

It wasn't long before we heard voices, then a curt laugh, and a sharp reprimand. We squatted and peered through the shrubbery. I detected half a dozen heavily armed men. I looked at Taylor, he was motionless and watched them closely. He grasped the shaft of his bow, he was wearing an archery armguard and a hand protector on his right hand, and his rifle hung from his left shoulder. I now understood why the Desert Rats feared him, he was an experienced adversary and knew his way around weapons.

Taylor raised his arm and motioned for us to stay. Then he stood and stepped on the path. One of the Desert Rats yelled and raised his gun, aiming it directly at Taylor.

"Stop!" Lars shouted. "I told you he was mine."

Seeing Lars and the Desert Rats filled me with intense anger, and I tasted bitterness in my mouth. I clenched my jaw and willed myself to remain calm. I was holding a loaded rifle and if the occasion arose, I was determined I would use it. To me it made no difference who I shot, I craved payback for Rusty.

"Taylor West," Lars growled. "You're a tough man to track."

Taylor stood motionless.

"You know why I came after you man, you stole from us; we want our guns and ammo back."

At this point, Taylor removed an arrow from the quiver, notched it to the bow string, then raised his arms and pointed it directly at Lars. "And you stole something belonging to us."

Lars snorted and shook his head. "Now what would a bunch of kids and misfits have worth stealing?"

"I plan on telling you," Taylor threatened in a steely voice. "Just before I release this arrow."

"Hey man, we go way back, I'll let you go after you return what's ours."

"That's the dilemma, Lars, you can't return what you took from us."

"You're talking crazy man; we don't have anything of yours."

"You've been tracking us from the Wastelands, and you know where we stopped and camped. The meadow with the huge willow, you didn't notice anything unusual?"

Before Lars could answer, a voice piped up. "That's the place we found the grave, Lars, there was a cross that had a name and some numbers on it."

Lars growled at the interruption, and Taylor turned and stared at the guy who spoke. "Bingo, you win the jackpot."

"Shit man," Lars replied, hatred crossing his face. "If I recall, you took out one of our guys, so as far as I'm concerned, we're even."

"You're telling me a terrified ten-year-old boy, shot through the heart, can be compared to the death of a blood-thirsty Neanderthal?"

The silence in the clearing was deafening. A few of the Desert Rats shuffled their feet, refusing to look at Taylor.

"Lars, you didn't say anything about a little kid getting killed," the guy who spoke earlier whined. "You said they took our weapons."

"They did, idiot, and that's the first I've heard anything about a kid," Lars answered heatedly, spinning to face the speaker.

Taylor spoke in a detached voice. "Your companion just mentioned you found the grave and the cross revealing the name and age of the little boy who died. Are you also telling me you didn't notice the blood in the train car?"

Lars turned and looked uncomfortably at Taylor, realizing if he made a wrong move, it would be his last. He glared at his men, observed the outrage on their faces and watched in astonishment as they lowered their arms.

"Why don't you disclose the real reason you led them on this goose chase, Lars? It wasn't because of the three rifles and a few rounds of ammunition; it was because you have a personal grudge against me, and you wanted pay-back."

Lars' face turned red with loathing, then he approached Taylor, who immediately tightened his bow, and without flinching, barked at Lars. "You have three seconds to step back, then I release this arrow. Do NOT push me, man."

"Come on Lars, let's go home," one of the guys behind him protested. "We'll call it square, no reason for a bunch of us getting killed for a couple of rifles and a few bullets."

Lars did not respond, and I noticed beads of perspiration on his forehead. He knew Taylor wasn't bluffing.

He lowered his rifle, then stepped back. "We'll let you go on one condition."

"What might that be, Lars."

"You got two girls with you; we want the brunette."

Taylor jerked visibly, lowered his bow, then simultaneously swung his rifle around and released the trigger guard. He moved slowly towards Lars and placed the barrel against his chest.

"You are a disgusting excuse for a human. Is this what you've become Lars, confiscating weapons and ammo, shooting innocent children, bargaining for women? You make me sick."

"You were the same when you led the Phantoms," Lars spat. "What makes you any different from me?"

The aggression between Taylor and Lars was fierce, and it was then I realized nothing would ever be solved between them until they challenged each other and one of them walked away the winner.

"The difference, Lars," Taylor emphasized in a resigned voice. "I left it all behind me, you didn't."

Then Taylor lowered his rifle, turned, and strolled towards us. Willie and I had our weapons aimed at Lars. Taylor pointed to the trigger guard and mimed how I was to release it. I stood frozen, unable to move.

"So, what now, West?" Lars demanded, staring angrily at Taylor's retreating back. "Do we write off everything, pretend nothing happened? You know I can't do that."

"It's personal, Lars," Taylor hissed angrily, turning to face him. "This is between you and me. Here's my proposal, I'll leave and swear I'll never come back. As far as I'm concerned, I can't leave here quick enough."

Lars sneered, then replied scornfully. "You come back; I'll kill you, West."

"You can try, do we have a deal?"

Lars nodded, then signalled to his men, who followed him into the bush. Taylor waited until they disappeared, then he stepped towards me, smiled, and took my rifle. He reached down and released the guard and handed it back to me.

"Aim your gun away from your foot and towards the ground in case it should accidentally go off; as soon as we're far enough away from here, put the trigger guard back on."

I nodded, and with a sigh of relief, followed Taylor into the shrubbery. I heard Willie's footsteps behind me.

"She most definitely needs to learn how to shoot a gun," I heard Tayor mutter to himself.

My legs were still shaking when we arrived where we left our supplies. The skirmish could have just as easily ended in tragedy.

We walked towards the bushes where Mai-Li and the kids hid. As instructed, she had found a flattened nest inside a juniper bush, probably made by a deer to hide her fawn. When she explained to Eddie and Debbie what it was, they were so delighted they moved right in. Mai-Li whispered to them to lower their voices a few times, reminding they were hiding. They eventually dozed off.

Taylor brought Mai-Li up to date on what happened during our confrontation with the Desert Rats.

"I know Lars swore he would go back to the Wastelands but are you positive you can trust him?" Mai-Li queried.

"No, not at all, but it got us out of this predicament."

"Why does he despise you so much?" I asked.

"There were a few issues back at Little Mountain I thought were resolved, yet it appears they weren't."

Mai-Li and I looked at each other, realizing Taylor was finished with his explanation, and for now it was all he was going to disclose.

We let the kids nap for another hour, then shook them awake, gave them some water and a cracker, and decided to put a few kilometres between us and the Desert Rats.

I stared at Taylor's back. Was he who he claimed to be, or was he acting a ruse, using us to hide his past? I knew I would not receive any peace until I talked with him, hoping to discover why he left the Phantoms and why there was so much animosity between him and Lars. I understood Taylor would speak only when he was ready and not before.

We hiked until dusk. Taylor backtracked twice and gave us the all-clear signal each time he returned. He confirmed the Desert Rats had turned around to begin their long trek back to the Wastelands. It was too late in the year for them to pursue us, snow was inevitable, and it would be fool hardy to continue their pursuit. The Desert Rats may have lost a few weapons and a man; our loss, was infinitely greater.

We found a protected grove, surrounded by Douglas and subalpine firs. The tents were set up, and Taylor started a campfire. Mai-Li surprised us with her long-awaited blueberry pancakes. I crushed half of the sugar cubes I received from the kind waitress in Hope, leaving a few for our coffee in the morning, and sprinkled them on top of the flapjacks.

We let the kids race around the clearing. Eddie was such a good sport, as Debbie always wanted to play with her ball, and he never told her no. Sometimes Willie would join them, and I usually stopped what I was doing and kept a keen eye on him. The kids enjoyed spending time with him, he would grab them around their ankles and spin them in circles, making them squeal in delight. I noticed he was extra cautious with Debbie, and I wondered if unintentionally he was beginning to care for her.

We were not far from the higher mountains, each day we lost more daylight, and the weather turned noticeably colder.

The sun rose later in the mornings and disappeared earlier at night. Hiking in the dark would be irrational, ferocious animals lived in the mountains, cougars, bears, coyotes, and wolves, to name a few, and we would be easy prey. There was always the possibility of clashing with humans as well, some of them more dangerous than any wild animal.

The kids were soon asleep, and the light from the campfire was comforting. I leaned against a tree, enjoying a cup of coffee sweetened by the last sugar cube. Mai-Li announced it was the last of the coffee as well. Then she told us she had an idea; she would substitute the coffee with chicory and asked us to be on the lookout for the plant, which normally grew until mid or late October. Because of the warmer weather we had experienced, a few late plants might still be around. She would need the roots and would prefer to pick them herself. I asked Mai-Li how chicory tasted, she smiled and returned to mending the kid's clothes. I should have realized her silence was an advanced warning.

Taylor, who had been listening to our conversation, drank the last of his coffee. Reaching inside his backpack he removed the map and spread it open on the ground. I spotted markings next to the mountains, creeks, and an occasional service road. We discussed the best route, and Taylor pointed out Sowaqua Creek and then trailed his finger down a dotted line and said it was the Hudson Bay Company or HBC Heritage Trail, which crossed several creeks and meadows. It was originally under the supervision of the Canadian Government, when the temperature changed, streams dried up and wildfires influenced the closure of many tourist accommodations, including the Trail. He believed he could find the path without too much difficulty, and hoped it was in half-decent shape for travelling. Unfortunately, any hostels or campsites provided for hikers were probably so rundown they would not be usable, or alternatively, were burned in wildfires.

Taylor folded the map and placed it inside his jacket pocket. He ran his fingers through his hair and told us he realized we would not make it to Princeton before it started snowing. He hoped to discover an abandoned hostel or a trapper's cabin to stay in for the winter. The next segment of our trek would be challenging, along with transporting provisions, backpacks, and weapons, most of our journey would be uphill.

A moody silence followed, then Taylor cleared his throat. "It's killing you, isn't it?" he asked, looking in my direction.

"What," I shrugged. Mai-Li smiled, and Willie had his usual smirk on his face.

"You've been aching to ask me all day why I left the Phantoms and what my history is with Lars?"

I stared at my cooling coffee. "Yeah, I guess we all should know why you left the head position of the largest and most powerful gang on Little Mountain and what your history was regarding Lars."

Taylor removed the coffee pot from the coals and poured the last dregs into his mug. He settled back against a tree trunk and swallowed. "I faced the same struggles as everyone else who survived the earthquake. I existed on my own, in abandoned houses, garages, whatever was available, and when the food disappeared, I moved on. I was always on the lookout for some low life bent on filching my provisions and weapons. I heard a lot of gossip about Little Mountain, so I decided to check it out for myself. One day while foraging, I ran across a large group, and immediately realized how hostile they were. They were heavily armed, displayed no fear, and eagerly eyed my backpack and rifle."

At this point, he took a drink and stared into the flames.

"One of the guys stepped forward and introduced himself as the leader of the Phantoms. The rest of his cronies circled me, snickering, reaching over to touch the barrel of my rifle. I was to either hand over all my possessions, and he would let me go unharmed, or I could fight for what I had. Understanding I was being offered an ultimatum, I questioned him if it was to be a battle between the two of us or, was I supposed to take on the whole gang.

"He advised it was between us, and none of the others were to interfere. Not knowing if his words were truthful, I seriously doubted I would be coming through this altercation in one piece. Realizing I had no choice, I set my supplies on the ground and removed my jacket. My holster and gun were strapped under my arm, and I spotted him eyeing them greedily as weapons were scarce. My archery equipment didn't interest him.

"I knew I would not survive if I lost this fight, as I sensed my challenger did not obey the same rules as the rest of his gang. He was all for himself, which made him unpredictable and dangerous.

"It was a long fight, and although my opponent was a big man, solid, and did not fight fair, I was stronger and in better shape. When it was over, he was lying unconscious on the ground. I picked up my provisions and turned to leave when the rest of the gang stood in a line blocking my exit. I watched them suspiciously, preparing for another encounter. One of them, probably the second in command, stepped forward and declared I was to finish the fight, then he reached over and grabbed my gun and pointed it at the fallen leader. 'You kill him, you're the new leader of the Phantoms.'

"I understood the code among the gangs. I just defeated their leader in a fight, now I must end it. I wasn't positive I wanted to accept their terms, but increasingly I was confronted by greedy individuals who coveted what I owned, and I knew it was only a matter of time before I was outnumbered, or someone who was a stronger fighter came along. I agreed on one condition. No more killing, the loser was to leave Little Mountain and never return. And that was how I became the leader of the Phantoms."

"The guy you defeated," I murmured. "It was Lars, wasn't it?"

Taylor nodded, not raising his head.

"Jeez, why did you leave the Phantoms, man?" Willie asked. "You had it made."

"I stayed, for over a year, as for having it made, I detested the way they existed, confronting other gang members who wanted to fight for my position and take what I owned. I heard through the grapevine Lars left Vancouver with a group and disappeared off the radar. It didn't take a genius to realize time was running out for all of us. Eventually, there would be another earthquake, or the volcano exploded, or the nuclear reactor plant in Washington blew up."

We turned and looked at each other.

Taylor noticed our raised eyebrows and confusion. "Believe me, it wouldn't take much for that to happen. The nuclear plant is less than four hundred kilometres from Vancouver, which was always an issue between Vancouver and Washington that it be modernized. Obviously, that never happened."

When none of us spoke, Taylor sighed. "Another topic, another time. I convinced the members of the Phantoms we needed to look elsewhere, our food supply was almost depleted, and the water was slowly drying up. The existing gangs were desperate, and if we stayed, none of us would survive. We split up and a few of us travelled north while the rest of us went to the Wastelands. That's where we discovered the old mining town and to my surprise, Lars. I gave him a lot of credit for surviving in such an inhospitable place. I assured him I did not care to fight him. We stayed with them for a few days, then returned to Vancouver. I completely misread Lars' sentiments towards me, obviously he was seeking revenge and desired to take control of the Phantoms again. You know the rest of the story, I walked away, handing the reins over to one of the other members. I wanted no part of it."

Taylor continued, staring directly at me. "I was on my own again until I met you in the sewer duct. I followed you as I needed to make sure you got back to the warehouse safely as I knew of two other gangs that were in the area and just as violent as the Phantoms. After straightening Willie out, I agreed to join your group, as your long-awaited Protector, of course."

Willie grunted, and I smiled at Mai-Li, who giggled, covering her mouth with her hands. We sat in silence for a while, staring at the dying coals.

"Unfortunately," Taylor added quietly. "Clashing with Lars and the Desert Rats when we took refuge in the train car was unexpected. It was then I realized his hatred for me had festered over time, and the rest, of course, is history. He took something very precious from us, and I will never exonerate him from that."

Taylor doused the fire, we all stood, and when he passed me on the way to his tent, he stopped and lightly caressed my cheek. I almost stumbled into the fire pit, he grabbed my arm, squeezed it lightly, and left.

Confused, I went to our tent, Mai-Li turned on her flashlight and we undressed and put on our PJs. I crawled inside my overnight bag, careful not to wake Eddie.

"Don't say a word," I murmured to Mai-Li when I noticed her watching me. I rolled over and closed my eyes. Then I heard, "Carlie has a boyfriend; Carlie has a boyfriend."

Then she turned off the light.

Chapter Five

We broke camp early the next morning. Our progress was leisurely, climbing steep hills and crawling over rockslides, I fretted more about Debbie than I did Eddie. She was not as agile as he and with her respiratory problems, she tired quickly. I noticed Mai-Li staring toward the mountains, and I knew she feared what lay ahead. At times, she had to coerce Debbie to keep moving.

By late afternoon, we arrived at Peers Creek Road, and Taylor decided it would be safer to travel following the stream. He remembered hiking through this area with his father years back; the road had been washed out and rockslides and washouts made it impassible and often they had been forced to backtrack.

We trudged for most of the day taking short breaks, until we arrived at the Sowaqua Creek Trailhead. We faced an open field, displaying evidence of heavy logging from years past. Deforestation and wildfires marred much of the beauty, adding to the destruction of hectares of trees and undergrowth.

We paced around the area and Willie shouted he found the remains of a campsite. We joined him and were surprised to see flat wooden platforms, some rotted beyond use, a few still usable.

"Carlie, what are those?" Eddie asked.

"They're platforms to set up our tents, that way we won't have to sleep on the ground. Cool huh?"

Eddie nodded, then sprinted off to tell Debbie his exciting news.

Taylor pointed to a huge, corroded drum half-buried in a deep hole. He pulled it out and discovered it was full of ashes and burnt wood. "Someone's been here not that long ago," he muttered, as he looked around the area. "We're not going to find anything better; we might as well set up camp."

I was glad he decided to stop. His aversion of coming across strangers was one of his major fears, and over time, we learned to trust no-one.

Sunset was not far off, reminding me again of the amount of daylight we were losing each day. After eating, Eddie and Debbie ran around the site. They seemed happier since Rusty's death and played more often.

I boiled water and loaded the water containers. Unaware of how many temperate days were left, Mai-Li and I took Debbie and Eddie down to the edge of the stream and washed them thoroughly. The water was chilly, and they complained bitterly, trying to escape. Two pouty, blue-lipped, shivering kids made their way back to camp. They told Taylor what happened, and he listened solemnly to their complaints.

"Well, kids, it's either a cold bath or you sleep outside with the wild animals?" he said. "It's your choice."

Debbie and Eddie gasped, looked at each other, and quickly scrambled inside the tent. I shook my head as I shuffled past Taylor. "Same goes for you, you know," he whispered. I snorted and left him standing outside in the dark.

The next morning, we left early. It was chilly and we made the kids put on their sweaters. I didn't want them to wear their gloves and coats yet, there would be colder days ahead.

A short hike later, we arrived at a conjunction where the stream converged with the trail. The footpath was furrowed and overgrown with grass and weeds. In the distance, we spotted a wooden bridge that crossed the creek, and the path disappeared into the dense forest. Yellow flower heads of goldenrods grew in abundance, as did blue chicory flowerets. Mai-Li was thrilled, and we helped her stuff one of the tote bags. If I'd known the taste of chicory before I picked it, I would not have been so eager to help.

I pointed to a white billboard leaning against a dilapidated shack. Eddie and I followed Taylor and waited as he studied it thoughtfully, then he pointed to dashes indicating a trail which wound around the east side of Mount Davis. It revealed a long, tough hike. It didn't look far to Princeton on the map but travelling through rugged country with two adolescent kids was slow, demanding, and could be dangerous. I understood Taylor's alarm and anxiety to keep all of us moving. The next leg of our journey would be through heavy bush and rugged mountain peaks, and if winter arrived early, finding a shelter was imperative, as we were not equipped to travel in snow.

Taylor shook his head and chuckled. "This is the same trail my dad and I hiked on years ago. I remember this place, brings back some happy memories."

"What kind of memories?" I questioned.

"Well, if you must know nosy parker, I snuck up behind my dad and splashed him with water. I laughed at him, and when he turned and looked at me, he was grinning wickedly, which was not a good sign. He chased me, but I could never outrun him. Usually, he tickled me until I gave in and apologized, but this time he picked me up and threw me into the stream."

Eddie's eyes were huge, absorbing Taylor's tale. "Debbie," he blurted as he ran to his friend. "Taylor's daddy threw him in this water right here when he was a kid." They both giggled and it was the most wonderful sound I'd heard in a long time.

Taylor, standing next to me, leaned over, and whispered. "It's improving, isn't it?"

I quickly looked away. "He sounds so much like his brother."

"True, he does, but Carlie, that's where the similarity ends. Eddie is serious and quiet, and our Rusty was impish, playful, and made us laugh."

I nodded and looked back at the kids. Mai-Li gave them each a drink of water. Then she glanced at the laces on their boots, for some reason Debbie's were always untied, and climbing over rocks, or forging through streams would be asking for disaster.

Taylor placed his arm around my waist, then leaned over and kissed my cheek. I did not pull away. "This is improving too?"

Then he picked up his bags and called us over to the path. "It's been years since I've been here. This is part of the Hudson Bay Heritage Trail, and it follows the east side of Mount Davis. Maybe we'll be lucky and spot a few animals or birds. I'm sure the kids would love seeing them."

"Just as long as it's not a bear," Willie snorted.

"I don't know," Taylor answered, turning to look at Willie. "I noticed you cuddling the bearskin a few days ago when you thought no one was looking."

"Asshole," he mumbled, staring angrily at Taylor.

I waited for it.

"Oh, oh, Willie swore," Eddie said. "No cookies for him tonight."

Everyone laughed, except Willie, then we gathered our belongings and took our positions in line, Eddie standing next to me. We started walking when suddenly Debbie stopped and pointed to the ground. "Look, it's a piece of wood, and it's got words on it."

Mai-Li knelt, the kids crowding around her. "It's an old sign, probably been here a long time." She picked it up and turned it over. "Hudson Bay Company (1849) Heritage Trail."

"Imagine finding this old sign," Taylor reflected, taking it from Mai-Li. "Let's set it back up, in case someone else comes this way, and they'll know which trail to take."

"Probably be another hundred years before that happens," Willie added. "You certain about the condition of the trail?" he questioned, looking at Taylor.

"No, I'm not, but it could be worse, we could be bushwhacking."

"Yeah, I guess so."

Taylor distractedly ran his fingers through his hair, then signalled for us to sit. "The safest way for us to travel is cross country, and I won't mince my words, the trail will be steep and demanding. Our progress will be strenuous, and we can't afford to make any mistakes. The first snowfall is not far off, so once we pass Mount Davis, we start looking for a cabin or shelter of some kind. Any questions?"

"Animal houses?" Debbie asked, raising her arm to gain Taylor's attention.

"Let's stay away from animal houses for a while, okay Debbie? The bears will be hibernating soon, and they shouldn't be disturbed."

"Cause a cranky bear is mean and dangerous," Eddie added.

"Got that right, guy. Now before we start, I have something important to say to you and Debbie. We are going to be climbing higher, so if you get tired," he turned and looked at Debbie, "or if you have trouble breathing, then you must tell someone. It's important, okay?"

Debbie nodded and took Mai-Li's hand. Eddie grabbed my jacket and leaned against me. I reached down and placed my hand on his head. "Don't worry, guy, I've got your back."

We all rose as one, taking our places in line. Eddie took my hand, and we headed down the weathered path and soon arrived at a wooden bridge. Some of the planks were rotted, and the side ropes were unravelled and worn. The river was high and roiling.

"This bridge crosses the Sowaqua Creek, and from the looks of it hasn't been used for a while. I'll go first," Taylor advised. "Wait until I arrive at the other side, and I'll signal if it's safe."

Shifting his gear and backpack to a more comfortable position, he stepped on the first rung, it creaked under his weight. When he arrived at the middle, he lowered his foot, unexpectedly the board cracked, and fell into the creek. I gasped, my heart pounding. He paused, then placed his weight on the next plank, then the next, and soon he was standing on the far side. Then he turned and gestured for the rest of us to follow.

Mai-Li chatted quietly to Debbie all the way across and guided her over the missing plank. Then it was my and Eddie's turn. We got to the far side with no problem, and I hugged Eddie and told him how brave he was. Then it was Willie's turn. He carried a heavy load, and when he stepped over the missing board and set his foot down on the plank, it cracked and fell into the water. His leg fell through the opening, and he quickly reached up and grabbed the side rope with both of his hands.

"Willie," Taylor shouted as he removed his gear and set it on the ground. "Keep perfectly still."

Without hesitation, I handed Eddie to Mai-Li, passed Taylor, stepped on the bridge, and shuffled slowly towards Willie. Taylor cursed softly and I knew I would have a lot of explaining to do. I removed two of Willie's bags to lighten his load and wrapped them around my neck. I then grabbed his arm and pulled him up. The surprised look on his face was almost comical. He steadied himself and followed me cautiously to the rest of the group.

"Why did you do that, Carlie?" Taylor snarled angrily when Willie and I stepped off the bridge.

"Because I'm a lot lighter than you, Taylor, the two of you would have fallen into the creek. I know you're both strong swimmers, but the last thing we need is wet provisions, it would take days to dry everything out and we can't afford any more delays."

"Sounds reasonable to me," Willie added.

"Bullshit," Taylor snorted, as he turned and looked directly at Willie. "We all know how much you hate taking baths."

Willie shrugged, not denying anything. I grinned, returned his supplies to him, and took my place in line.

"We're still not finished talking about this Carlie," Taylor mouthed, as he strolled past me to the front of the line. "Let's make tracks."

The heavy rain in the area had caused severe damage over time. We spotted evidence of mud and rockslides and circumvented holes in the middle of the path. We came across trickling streams and easily jumped across. I stopped Debbie from removing her sweater, explaining she would catch a cold if she got chilled. She turned to look at Mai-Li, who nodded in agreement. "Sorry, Debbie, Carlie's right. The higher we climb the colder it's going to become."

Before Debbie could cause a scene, Eddie handed her Squishy. Peace was restored, at least for now.

The forest was populated with bewitching-pines, cedars, and birch which grew in crowded clusters, the ground was hidden under ferns and vegetation. I smelled smoke in the distance and mentioned it to Willie.

"Wildfires," he said. "There are more of them all the time; hundreds of thousands of hectares of forests have disappeared, which unfortunately increases our chances of coming across rockslides, and later in the season, avalanches. The saving redemption is that the cooling temperatures and snow should slow down the burning."

I stared at Willie in bewilderment, it wasn't often I heard him providing input about any topic. I must have caught him at a weak moment.

Eventually, the trees thinned, and we arrived at a meadow. Exposed slopes were covered in burdock bushes and withered wildflowers. The views were stunning as we gazed at distant mountains. In dismay, I noted snow covering the higher reaches.

"Okay," Taylor explained. "This is Mount Davis Trail, and it circumvents the east side of Mount Davis. I know it's been a long day, but I believe there's another campsite halfway down the trail we can stop at for the night."

At one point, the path disappeared, and we stood in a huddle as we faced a meadow that ended at the base of an enormous hill. Taylor used the compass to ensure we were headed in the right direction. The meadow was flat, and the scenery was impressive. The kids laughed and chased each other. The hill, unfortunately, was a strenuous climb, and my legs ached from the unaccustomed workout. I pulled an elastic band from my pocket and twisted my hair in a knot.

We finally arrived at the bottom of the slope and sighed in relief when we spotted the path again. It was level, making it easier to walk.

We resumed our journey, followed the mountain, and stopped around noon. Eating a light lunch, we encouraged the kids to drink a lot of water as it would be easy for them to get dehydrated. We passed several streams along the way, and I hoped to come across others higher up the mountain.

After a short rest, we were once again on the trail. We travelled along a steep ridge, and I made Eddie stay on the side away from the edge. A few hours later we arrived at a different meadow, and I spotted a stream in the distance. Huge boulders were scattered around the moor.

"I believe this is Conglomerate Flats, I read it on the poster at the trailhead," Taylor commented. "Should be tent platforms around here somewhere."

Mai-Li pointed towards the open field, where an old bench made from planks and tree trunks was located.

"Can we go see," Eddie asked Mai-Li.

"Go ahead," she said. "Just make sure you stay in sight, don't wander off."

The kids jumped in excitement and took off; I smiled at their enthusiasm.

I removed my backpack and bags and set them on the ground. "Mai-Li, I'm going to climb this knoll and see if there are any platforms in the area."

I soon reached the top and marvelled at the beauty of the distant mountains and valleys. Again, I spotted plumes of smoke burning in the distance. I searched the overgrown meadow, then looked down. A few well-protected platforms were located on the far side of the slope, Taylor and Willie must have wandered right past them.

"Taylor," I shouted. He turned and lifted his head, catching sight of me on top of the incline.

I pointed downwards. "There are platforms at the bottom of this hill, although I can't make out what sort of shape they're in. Bring the kids back with you."

He waved, then he and Willie headed back, collecting Eddie and Debbie on their way.

Suddenly a gust of frigid wind almost blew me over. I watched as an ominous black cloud headed directly towards us. We needed to find shelter as quickly as possible, if we were caught in the open in the middle of a rainstorm, it would take days for everything to dry.

I side-stepped down the grade, then grabbed as many of the bags and packs I could carry and headed for the platforms. Mai-Li chased after me, and I shouted at her to bring the rest of the supplies.

Taylor and Willie were looking at the platforms, and I realized we didn't have time to be fussy.

"A powerful thunderstorm is headed this way. Set up the small tent and put the supplies inside. Take out what we'll need tonight. Mai-Li and I will set up the big tent."

Taylor nodded, and he and Willie quickly installed the tent on the nearest platform, wrestling with it while the wind blew violently, causing the sides to flap wildly. Mai-Li and I struggled as we set up the larger tent, then grabbed the supplies Taylor and Willie had chosen for the night. Mai-Li took Debbie inside, and I told her I would join them shortly.

I gestured for Eddie to help me gather rocks, which we placed around the edges of the small tent. When Taylor and Willie saw what we were doing, they did the same for the larger tent. The wind picked up, the temperature dropped, and I shivered in my light coat. I was glad I had insisted earlier the kids wear their heavier sweaters and mittens.

We climbed inside the big tent, at once followed by Taylor and Willie. We zipped it close, and almost immediately, the skies opened, the rain fell in huge drops, pounding on the ground and the tent.

Mai-Li spread three of the overnight bags on the floor. "This is a perfect location for the tents," Taylor remarked. "The hill is an effective buffer from the wind, which I suppose blows frequently up here."

"No heated supper tonight," Mai-Li let us know as she handed around two opened cans of brown beans. "I've been saving these for a special treat, this is the last of them, so enjoy."

Everyone groaned. We each ate our share, and when the beans were gone, Mai-li gave everyone an Oreo cookie.

"Oh, by the way," she added. "These are ......"

"I know, I know," interrupted Eddie. "These are the last of the Oreos, so enjoy them."

We all roared, I was chewing on my cookie and choked. Taylor reached over and pounded my back. The kids thought it was hilarious and laughed louder.

Aware the storm might take a while to pass, I pulled the comics from my backpack. Willie dove for the closest ones, while the kids grabbed what was left.

"Carlie," Eddie asked. "How come you have all the comics and crayons in your pack? We can carry some of them."

"Thanks, guys, I don't mind."

"You don't even read comics," Eddie commented.

"Willie does."

Eddie's face went blank.

"So, think about it," I hinted.

"I know, I know," Debbie shouted excitedly. We all turned as one and looked at her.

Mai-Li nodded, and Debbie shouted as loudly as she could. "Cause, Willie would read the comics all the time, and he wouldn't keep up with us and he would get lost or fall off the mountain, and we would never find him again."

That got everybody laughing again, except Willie of course. "Jeez, now you have Debbie making fun of me. Nice going."

"Oh Willie," I replied. "It's all in fun."

"Willie," Debbie interjected." It's okay, I like you. You're my friend."

Willie's face flushed, then he leaned against his pack, opened the comic, and forgot any of us existed.

We let the kids skim through the comics Willie had not confiscated, and I gave each of them a piece of paper and crayons. They settled down, and we were cozy and comfortable.

The wind howled persistently, and the rain fell heavily. The sides of the tent snapped sharply, and at times I wondered if the pegs would hold. I spoke quietly to the kids and helped them with their drawings; I should never have let them know I knew how to draw.

Taylor took out his map to confirm our route for the next day. He frowned, refusing to look at me. I realized he was still annoyed when I rescued Willie on the bridge, but I did not regret my spontaneous decision.

At times we were forced to set up an early camp, often when Taylor was not ready to stop. I hoped he would eventually accept we could not travel long hours with the kids though such harsh terrain. We couldn't chance the risk of injury, as they tired easily and did not have the resilience the rest of us had.

Taylor was unmistakably the leader of our group, but at times he took on more than he could manage.

Debbie stopped colouring and asked Mai-Li if she could throw her ball tomorrow, and she told her not until we reached the bottom of the mountain. If it rolled over the side, it would be gone forever.

"Willie can find it for me."

"I'm not a goat, Debbie," Willie replied, lowering his comic. Mai-Li grinned and looked at me. Since he carried Debbie to safety during the firestorm, she had lost her fear of him and now thought of him as her friend.

"Your name sounds the same as a goat," Debbie giggled.

Willie looked at her vaguely.

"Cause, your name is Willie, and a boy goat's name is Billie."

Willie sighed heavily, then returned to his reading.

I looked around the tent, and knew the kids were content, Mai-Li was at peace, Willie was engrossed reading the comics, and Taylor was watching me. My face reddened, and I quickly turned away.

"We might as well make up the beds, it's going to be dark soon, and I don't want to use the flashlights if we don't have to," Taylor said. "Unfortunately, there's not going to be a lot of room. Keep your clothes on, it's going to be cold tonight."

We placed Eddie and Debbie in the middle, then Mai-Li and I lay on one side, and Taylor and Willie stretched out on the other. The bear skin was tossed over the kids.

"Story, Carlie," Debbie asked. I was ready to make an excuse when Taylor intervened. "Sounds like a good idea to me, Debbie."

I raised my head and scowled. Taylor grinned and lay back, Willie was already snoring, and the kids waited for me to start my "nighttime story," as Debbie called it.

I snuggled inside my overnight bag, contented and at peace, aware Taylor understood I was no longer in my dark place, the ache in my heart was healing, and I was once again part of the group.

Chapter Six

The next morning, we examined the damage. One of the ropes from the smaller tent broke loose, thankfully the rain did not leak inside, and the supplies were intact.

Huge puddles of water covered the ground, I spotted a few downed trees, the shrubs and plants were flattened by the heavy downpour. The air was crisp, and I rubbed my hands together and warmed them. It was always a worry that lightning would start new wildfires, fortunately cooler temperatures and heavy rains kept them under control.

Taylor started a campfire, and Mai-Li brewed a pot of chicory. The first time I tasted it, I almost choked. I never acquired a taste for the bitter brew, despite the fact the rest of them appeared to enjoy it. The one saving salvation was that it was hot and kept the morning chill away.

While Mai-Li was preparing porridge and hot chocolate for the kids, I took the water container and canteen and headed towards the far side of the field. The day before, when I climbed the hill behind the platforms, I spotted a brook bordering the tree line. I heard footsteps behind me and turned sharply. Taylor caught up to me, and I slowed my pace.

"You don't need to come with me," I snapped irritably. "The stream is not far from here."

"It's okay, I don't mind."

"You're assuming I'll get into trouble? Is that why you brought your bow with you?"

"I always carry a weapon wherever I go, I know you'll be okay, it's just that Eddie was worried."

"What for?"

"He suggested I keep an eye on you, and if a lion or a bear attacks, I'm supposed to jump on you and save you."

"That's crazy, when I return to camp, I'm going to speak to him about it."

"He's just concerned about you."

"I know."

"Besides, the idea of jumping on you sounds appealing."

I sighed, turned, and continued strolling. "As long as you behave yourself, you can join me."

"I don't really have much choice, do I?" Taylor mumbled.

We eventually arrived at the stream, and I handed the canister to Taylor. "Here, make yourself useful."

Soon we were headed back to camp. Taylor reached over and took the canteen I was lugging; I shook my head, and he smiled and returned it to me. I had made a promise to myself I would do my share of the work, although I silently admitted I was relieved he was carrying the heavier container.

Mai-Li was just dishing up the food, and I got the water pot from our supplies, filled it, and put it on the coals to boil.

We ate leisurely, enjoying the porridge. The kids inhaled their chocolate, and I wished I were drinking that instead of chicory. Ever since Mai-Li told us chicory was loaded with Vitamins A and C and listed all its benefits, there was no way we could refuse a cup every morning.

We waited until the boiled water cooled enough to fill the water container and the canteen. Then we packed, took down the tents, and left.

The trail was narrow, muddy, and slippery. We moved in single file. If we approached a steep drop on one side, I made Eddie grab hold of my belt and trail as close to me as possible. It worked well, and I wasn't as nervous.

We hiked for half an hour when unexpectedly I felt dizzy and lost my balance. The ground shook, and rocks and dirt rolled down the side of the mountain and onto the path. Taylor shouted for us to stop and to stay away from the edge. As quickly as it started, the tremors stopped.

My stomach tightened and I fought back nausea. I inhaled slowly, battling my inherent fear of earthquakes and tremors.

Eddie wrapped his arms around my waist, and I held him tightly.

"Was that an earthquake?" Willie questioned from the back of the line.

"I don't believe so, it wasn't powerful enough," Taylor answered. "With all the seismic activity in the area, there are a lot of tremors and shocks. Let's keep going and if we experience another one, move as far away from the edge as possible."

We hiked for hours; traipsing on the slick trail was difficult and nerve-wracking, especially when there was a chance of more tremors. At times I wished we could cut through the forest, which wouldn't have been practical as it would add hours to our travelling time, and we couldn't take a chance of losing our way.

At one point, I spotted in the distance an extensive area of scorched trees. Taylor had stopped on the trail and noticed where I was looking. "That's part of the damage done by the 2023 wildfire," he muttered.

"2023?"

"It takes a long time for regrowth, especially firs and cedars, up to 150 years for them to reappear. Birch, aspen, spruce, and pine grow slightly faster, but we won't see them in our lifetime."

"Did people burn the trees down?" Eddie enquired.

"Sometimes, by carelessness," Taylor answered. "Lightning strikes and climate change had a lot to do with it as well. With the temperatures becoming hotter all the time, it doesn't take much for a fire to start."

I shook my head dejectedly. What a legacy we were leaving behind.

I shivered as an icy updraft blew from the valley, and spotted dark, threatening clouds and hoped it wouldn't start raining again. Considering our recent conversation about wildfires, maybe I should welcome the moisture.

Changing the subject, I pointed out the peak of a mountain in the distance and Eddie asked me what its name was. I told him I didn't know, and Mai-Li, who was in front of us, overheard our conversation.

'That's Tulameen Mountain, Eddie, it's a long way from here."

"Are we goanna go to that place, Mai-Li?" Debbie asked.

"No, Debbie, it's north of us, and we are headed east. Eddie, maybe one day when you are older, Taylor or Carlie can take you there. It's not an easy climb, it's surrounded by heavy forests, with lots of rock and steep grades, but when you reach the summit you can see mountains in every direction."

Eddie nodded enthusiastically, and I expected Taylor would hear all about it after we stopped and set up camp.

Nervously, I motioned Eddie to stay away from the edge, we rounded a bend on the path and stopped in our tracks. An enormous pile of dirt and sediment had buried the path; I quickly grabbed Eddie's sleeve and shifted him closer to the wall.

Taylor instructed us to not move, then he cautiously approached the debris. He knelt and slowly moved a few rocks, then rose, turned, and faced us.

"It's a recent rockslide, probably caused by the seismic activity we recently felt, with a little help from last night's rainstorm. The ground water saturated the soil and the extra weight and the latest shocks we just experienced triggered the slide."

"Do we turn around and find a different route, Taylor?" Mai-Li asked.

"Let me take a closer look, Mai-Li, and if it's stable, we'll climb over, otherwise, we will have to backtrack and find another route. It will add time to our journey, but we can't take any unnecessary risks."

Taylor removed his backpack, supplies and weapons and placed them on the path. Then he cautiously climbed the rubble, stopping abruptly when rocks dislodged and rolled over the edge.

After what seemed an eternity, he arrived at the far side of the slide. "We should be able to cross here, I'm coming back, and I'll take Eddie and Willie you bring Debbie; leave their backpacks, we need to concentrate on keeping them calm. Carlie, you, and Mai-Li cross behind us once we're on the far side. Carry your own equipment and if you can manage the kid's packs bring them with you, leave them if you feel overloaded. Willie and I will come back for the rest.”

Taylor cautiously manoeuvred back to our small group. He smiled at Eddie, who released my arm.

“You ready, big guy?” Taylor asked.

Eddie nodded, turned, and looked at me, then took Taylor’s hand. “No, but go ahead anyway.”

Taylor instructed Eddie to step carefully and to follow him closely. I gasped as sediment and rocks rolled down the slide and over the side of the mountain. It wasn’t long before they reached their destination. By now Willie was standing beside Debbie, who was clutching his hand. “Can you piggyback me, Willie?”

“Not this time, Debbie, we have to pay attention so we don’t fall, okay?”

“Don’t follow the same path I did,” Taylor instructed. “We don’t want to loosen additional rocks and trigger another slide.”

Willie nodded and climbed the steep grade, pausing when Debbie stopped. I was amazed at his patience with the young girl, he unquestionably did not use the same constraint with Eddie or the rest of us. They joined Taylor and Eddie, Debbie waved, and Mai-Li and I waved back.

“Alright ladies,” Taylor commanded.

Mae-Li grabbed her backpack and Debbie’s, which was bulkier than Eddie’s, and her basket of medicines and herbs. Realizing she was toting too heavy a load, I took the basket, along with my pack and Eddie's, and struggled up the rockslide, remembering not to follow in Mai-Li's tracks. We clawed our way upwards, stopping often to catch our breath. I was aware of the importance of Mai-Li's precious basket as we all relied heavily on her medicines and herbs.

We arrived safely and slid gingerly down the scree. Taylor and Willie at once returned to the far side, and quickly joined us with the rest of the packs, supplies, and weapons.

"Terrific job everyone," Taylor praised. "Let's keep moving, I believe we're almost at the bottom of the trail."

We strode steadily downhill, which for some reason seemed to be more strenuous for me than climbing up. The path eventually flattened, and we picked up our pace.

The kids were tiring, and we stopped a few times when Debbie wheezed, struggling to catch her breath. The daylight gradually dissipated, we needed to find a place to make camp for the night. We had passed two creeks flowing northwest and I was thankful for the continuous supply of water.

We turned a corner when Taylor and Mai-Li stopped abruptly. I pulled Eddie backwards before he crashed into them.

"Watch out, Willie," I cried, turning to see how close he was. His head was down, and he almost ploughed into us.

In front of us was a road. Impressions of furrows, probably left by a cart or tire tracks a long time ago, indicated it was once well-travelled. Over time, the weeds took over.

Taylor gestured for Willie to join him, and Mai-Li and I steered the kids into the underbrush. We signalled them to crouch down, we did not have to tell them to be quiet.

Taylor and Willie disappeared. They soon returned, and we joined them in the open. Taylor was holding his map. "We're still on the Hudson Bay Heritage Trail," he affirmed, pointing to our location. "However, this road is not shown. I'm curious to find where it leads, we might discover a protected spot to set up camp for the night. Okay kids, do we turn left or right, you decide."

Eddie leaned over the map, then rubbed his chin, deep in thought, and Debbie copied him. I looked at Mai-Li and grinned.

"Let's go left," Eddie decided.

"Yeah, left," Debbie shouted happily.

Taylor nodded, and we left the trail; we hiked for about ten minutes, when the road abruptly vanished and turned back into a narrow path.

"That explains why it's not documented on the map," declared Taylor, "It was never completed."

We picked up our pace, my back and legs were stiff and sore. I didn't worry about the kids, they appeared to have more energy than the rest of us. I was about to suggest we stop for the night as I didn't want to set up the tents in the dark.

We rounded a corner and froze. Before us was a log cabin with rickety steps leading to a covered porch that swept across the front and down the right side. An attached room had been built on the left side of the cabin, and under an enormous cedar a few metres to the left was a dilapidated outhouse.

"Willie, bring your gun and come with me. The rest of you keep low and stay hidden until I give the all-clear. You know the drill."

Willie dropped his bags, and quickly joined Taylor. Mai-Li and I motioned the kids to lay flat on the ground.

A brief time later, Taylor shouted. "It's okay, the place is empty; doesn't look as if it's been used for a long time. Just leave our bags, we'll get them."

The kids stood and I adjusted Eddie's backpack. We passed the guys on their way back to retrieve their supplies. We arrived at the cabin; the door was ajar. Mai-Li instructed Eddie and Debbie to stand at the bottom of the steps and wait for Taylor and Willie. Then we climbed the creaky steps, and cautiously opened the door all the way and stepped inside; it was a dump. Spider webs hung from the ceiling and shrouded the windowpanes. Most of the furniture was destroyed and an old wood burning stove was turned on its side with ashes scattered around the room.

I wandered over to the cupboard and opened a door. I screamed as a dark and furry animal jumped out, hit me squarely on my chest, landed on the floor and tore out the front exit. Taylor charged inside and looked anxiously around.

"What happened?" he sputtered, looking directly at me; it didn't take a genius to notice my flushed face and realize I was the one causing the commotion.

"I opened the cupboard door, and a packrat jumped on me."

"Lucky rat," Taylor mumbled. Then he turned and joined Willie and the kids outside.

Mai-Li chuckled softly, and I gave her a scathing look, as I investigated inside the cupboard to see if our resident had left any presents. Its nest was padded with bones, foliage, and a few unidentifiable objects.

"It took me by surprise," I murmured, more to myself than May-Li. "I hate rats."

"We'll leave the cupboard as it is for now, in case we decide to move on," Mai-Li chuckled. "If we should, there's a likely chance your friend will return."

Taylor and Willie soon joined us, and we asked where the kids were. "They're sitting on the porch steps," Taylor answered. "I told them to stay there, no sense having them walk through this mess."

The four of us stood in the middle of the room. I looked at Mai-Li, who was possibly having the same worrying thoughts as me.

"I wonder whose house this is," I muttered. "Although it doesn't look as if anyone has lived here in a long time."

"That may be true, but someone has been using it and not that long ago, they left it in disgusting shape," Mai-Li answered critically. "Hopefully they won't return."

I looked at her, understanding her concern. The train car in the Wastelands brought back too many unwanted memories for both of us.

Taylor wandered around the room, then bent down, and examined the overturned wood stove. He salvaged a flue buried in a pile of garbage and laid it next to the heater.

"The cabin is well built," he muttered, more to himself than the rest of us. "The stove is in decent shape, hopefully there's a stovepipe chimney around somewhere, and with a little luck, it might work."

"Do you think there's a chance we can stay, Taylor?" I asked.

"If the wood burner can be fixed. We won't know until we take a closer look at the rest of the place. It's almost dark, let's set up the tents and get some sleep."

The kids rose quickly when we joined them on the porch. Mai-Li and I installed the tents and set up the bedrolls while the kids raced around the yard.

The guys headed into the trees to gather wood and kindling for the campfire. Mai-Li dealt with the cooking while I joined the kids. Debbie was so wound up she threw her ball into the bushes, and we went through a few anxious moments until it was found.

I wasn't sure if I was thrilled or alarmed about discovering the abandoned homestead. The thought of trying to survive here through the winter was daunting. How I wished we'd left Vancouver two months earlier as we would have been in Blackfoot by now. I knew it was impractical dwelling on what might have been and accepted the fact it would be foolhardy and dangerous to continue our journey through the mountains this late in the year.

Our current food supply should last for a few more weeks, and hopefully, Taylor and Willie would have luck hunting, and we would have meat to tide us over for a while.

Mai-Li summoned everyone to the fire. She heated bear stew for everyone and gave a cracker to each of the kids.

"I apologize about the taste of the stew, but I couldn't locate the berries."

"What berries Mai-Li?" Taylor inquired.

"I've been picking blueberries and cranberries ever since we left the Wastelands, and I collected a full bag, now I can't find it anywhere."

"We'll help look tomorrow; it's almost dark and it's been a long day. Maybe it got placed in the wrong backpack."

"I hope so, otherwise there won't be any more this year. I use them to add flavour to the stews, and I give the kids a handful every morning, they're rich in Vitamin C and can cure lots of ailments. How could I have been so careless?"

"Don't beat yourself up," I exclaimed. "You're too vigilant to have lost them, Taylor's right. It's around here someplace."

We undressed the kids and tucked them in their sleeping bags. The rest of us strolled outside and sat around the campfire, sipping hot chicory. We were exhausted and it would be an early night for all of us.

"First thing in the morning," Taylor told. "We'll check the cabin and the area, right now I'm turning in."

He and Willie headed towards the other tent, and Mai-Li and I doused the flames and gathered the cups. It didn't take me long to doze off.

The next morning, after we ate, Taylor wandered to the cabin. The kids raced around the yard, and we kept a close watch on them, warning them to stay close as there were still bears around.

I gave Mai-Li a hand unpacking the food rations, and we spread them on the tarp, Willie dozed with his back propped against a tree trunk, and I shook him awake and told him perhaps he could join Taylor in the cabin. He grumbled, stood, and glared at me, and the look on his face made me recoil. A nagging suspicion about the missing berries filled my head and I prayed I was wrong, silently scolding myself for being so paranoid. His attitude towards me had improved somewhat since leaving the meadow; I did not want to aggravate him and cause dissention in the group.

Mai-Li and I determinedly rummaged for the berries. However, our search was futile, and I helped a miserable Mai-Li put everything back in its place. I suggested we join Taylor and see if he were ready to make a decision as to whether we would be spending the winter here.

We entered the cabin, leaving the door open so we could watch the kids. They had discovered a hole filled with water and entertained themselves making mud pies. If we decided to stay, I wondered if a creek was close by.

Taylor spotted us and climbed over a pile of discarded wood and trash, he joined us by the front door, which was the only uncluttered space available. He was covered in dirt and spiderwebs; Willie had disappeared.

"Any luck ladies?" he questioned.

Mai-Li shook her head, and I knew the disappearance of the berries still bothered her and would probably bother her for a long time.

"We're always in such a rush to pack and start moving, it wouldn't be hard to miss something."

"I've thought of that Taylor," Mai-Li replied. "I recall yesterday morning I had packed them, and the only thing I can think of is I must have dropped the bag on the trail, although if I did Carlie or Eddie should have spotted it right away."

"Maybe we lost it when we climbed over the rockslide, Mai-Li," I suggested. "I carried your basket, and it might have fallen out then."

Mai-Li shrugged, and I turned and faced Taylor. "Okay, what's the verdict, do we stay or do we leave?"

"The walls and roof are sound, some of the windowpanes are smashed, they need to be boarded over, which is an effortless fix. Our main concern is the wood-burning stove which needs to be scrubbed, and the flue reinstalled. There's plenty of fuel in the area, we're surrounded by trees. I'll look at it first thing tomorrow morning and we can make our decision then."

"Do you think we are trespassing on someone's claim?" Mai-Li asked.

Taylor shook his head. "Aside from the hikers passing through and leaving their garbage behind, no-one's been living here for a while, I found a miner's claim, it suffered a lot of water damage and is hard to read. I estimate it's over a hundred years old."

"I grew up hearing about the deserted cabins in these mountains, built by miners and trappers who came to strike it rich," Mai-Li recalled. "Blackfoot, the place where my family now live, was once a goldrush town. Over ninety cottages were built before it was eventually abandoned. At least half of the people were Chinese. They were treated terribly; they could only prospect on abandoned claims. Their key role was to provide services to the townspeople, operating grocery stores and laundries. Their names were never recorded, and those who died were buried in unmarked graves."

Taylor and I listened solemnly. He shook his head despondently. "Your ancestors faced insurmountable hardships, and when the miners moved on, I assume they remained and made Blackfoot their home."

"That is true."

"They sound resourceful and resilient, making a difference in a positive way, leaving the world a better place. You must be proud of your heritage."

Mai-Li nodded perceptively. "I remember years ago when my family visited our grandparents, we were told about the history of Blackfoot. I know you have a passion for history, and I look forward introducing you to my family, Taylor West."

Taylor's face reddened; compliments always made him uncomfortable. Abruptly, he changed the topic and pointed towards the debris scattered around the room.

"Okay, there's dirt and garbage to be disposed of. We also found a squirrel's nest inside the stove, Carlie can remove it, she took care of the packrat with no problem."

Mai-Li snickered, and I made a face at him.

Taylor stood in the middle of the room, turning in a circle. "Raccoons have moved into the shed, and they're not as easy to dispose of as a packrat, we'll let Willie do it. If we all pitch in, and with a lot of persistent work, we can make do."

Suddenly, Taylor turned and faced me. "Where's Willie?"

Shaking my head, I looked towards Mai-Li. "He was outside a few minutes ago, snoring loudly," she replied. "Carlie woke him and suggested he join you here. He didn't show up?"

Taylor shook his head. "Haven't seen him in ages. Where are the kids?"

I went to the door and pointed outside, and we all hooted. Debbie's hair, face, jeans, and sweater were caked in mud. Eddie looked as if he just taken a bath. When the kids heard us, and realized they had a captive audience, they bombarded us with flying projectiles of mud.

Jumping back, I shook my head and without thinking, said. "Remember you have to wash your own clothes if you make them dirty."

Eddie grinned, Debbie looked down at her shirt and jeans, screwed up her face and started to cry. Mai-Li ran to her, took her in her arms, and tried to console her.

"Oh man," I muttered, slumping my shoulders. "I did it again."

Taylor leaned over and kissed me. I pulled away. "I swear, if I ever have kids of my own, I'm leaving their upbringing to their father."

"Good to know," Taylor whispered.

Realizing what I just said, I made a quick beeline outside, smacking solidly into Willie. I had no idea how long he was standing nearby; he must have been listening behind the door. A queasiness filled my stomach. I stepped around him and headed towards Mai-Li and the kids.

My flushed face was a dead giveaway. Mai-Li smiled. Eddie was watching me closely and although at times our relationship was fragile, it was improving daily. I often wondered what he was sensing, as I realized he was aware of the growing tension between me and Taylor.

"Let's wash the kids first," I suggested to Mai-Li. "Taylor wants to have a group meeting."

Mai-Li quickly stripped Debbie and found jeans and a top for her to wear and dug out an old cloth to wipe her face and hair.

We wandered back to the cabin. Willie and Taylor were reassembling the wood stove and were at the point of connecting the flue. Taylor wiped the dirt off his hands. "It's filthy in here, let's go back to the tent."

Soon the six of us were seated on the bedrolls. I sensed something was off. I looked around, positive I had placed the Oreo cookies next to the porridge and crackers, yet now they were beside Mai-Li's herb basket. Willie was watching me, almost as if he dared me to say something. The last thing I needed was to quarrel with him. We had to make it through the winter, with another long hike before we reached Princeton. And, as much as I despised admitting it, at times he was useful, helping Taylor lug heavier supplies and share with the physical labour.

"Okay, let's go over this," Taylor began. "We found this place, which needs a lot of TLC should we decide to stay here for the winter."

Taylor noticed the kids looking at each other, and he smiled. "TLC means tender loving care, does that make sense?"

"Yup," Eddie answered. "It means we have to clean it up really nice so we can live in it."

Taylor nodded. "There's a definite change in the temperature at night, and I wouldn't be surprised if it snows in the next few days."

"Snowman," Debbie squealed, flinging her arms upward.

"And snowball fights," Eddie added in an ominous voice.

The rest of us weren't quite as enthusiastic as the kids, which made me wonder about the obstacles we would be facing. "Before we make a final decision," I asked, turning to look at Taylor. "What do you consider our chances are if we tried to hike over the pass, and to the highway, assuming it hasn't started snowing?"

"I understand your question, it would definitely cut a lot of time off our journey," Taylor answered. "Unfortunately, the trail becomes steeper, and we have a long, gruelling climb in front of us. The mountains east of here are not as high as Mount Davis, however we still need to traverse around them. Several creeks are in the area, and I'm not definite how much rain there's been, there is a possibility we might not be able to ford them. According to the map, we'll eventually arrive at a service road, which trails the east side of Lodestone Mountain. The road improves somewhat once we pass through the Tanglewood Hills. But that's a long way from here, and we are gambling it doesn't snow."

"That is true, Taylor, and the trail you mentioned eventually arrives at Coalmont Road, which leads into Princeton," Mai-Li added.

"Ah," Taylor said, "We are in your neighbourhood."

"It has been a long time since I have been here. My father used to take me and my brothers hiking in the Tanglewood Hills. The Tanglewood Mine was one of the most lucrative iron, magnetite, and titanium mines in the Interior, unfortunately the wildfires and economy forced it to shut down. I have no notion what condition the path is in right now, it was not well travelled, and is in uninhabited country, with many wild animals."

"What sort of animals?" Eddie questioned eagerly.

"Bears, moose, deer and cougars, wolves, coyotes, just to name a few."

"Something else to think about when the time comes," Taylor said. "However," he proclaimed turning to face me and Mai-Li, "We need to decide whether we stay here for the winter or keep moving, and I might add, finding another lodging before it starts snowing is highly unlikely."

"Okay, another alternative to staying here, what if we leave and put in as many kilometres as we can," I queried. "Let's say it hasn't snowed yet, and we arrive at Coalmont Road, instead of going to Princeton, which heads north, we hike to Blackfoot instead?"

Mai-Li frowned. "Carlie, why are you suggesting we go to Blackfoot, I thought we planned on going to Princeton first?"

"That route adds a lot of extra travelling time, and I know how anxious you are to be with your family. Dropping you off first makes more sense."

"As I have mentioned before, all of you are welcome to stay in Blackfoot. I worry that Princeton might not be a safe place to take young children. It is no different than any of the other towns we passed in our travels."

"I understand your questions, Carlie, it's good to look at all alternatives before we make a final decision. However, there is another problem we haven't discussed,"

Taylor answered, shaking his head. "I don't assume it would be safe hiking next to the highway as I imagine conditions are no different than other roads we travelled on. Our best solution is to stay on the trails, which would increase our walking distance and travelling time."

"Do we stay, or do we go?" Willie questioned sharply.

"As I mentioned," Taylor answered. "We need to vote. I feel we should stay here; we don't want to get caught in heavy snow. This place would be a lot safer and warmer than wintering in a cave or animal den. Willie, how about you?"

"We should go."

Taylor pressed his lips tightly, then frowned, and I sensed he was annoyed at Willie's abrupt decision.

"I think we should stay," Mai-Li replied.

Five faces turned and faced me. Willie was watching me sharply. I did not hesitate to make my decision; the kids came first.

"I think you are right about the imminent arrival of snow," I said, turning to face Taylor. "We have no choice, we stay."

"That doesn't surprise me," Willie angrily interrupted, staring me down. "He's got you on a pretty tight leash?" Then he flung the tent flap open and left.

Taylor's jumped up and headed towards the exit.

"Taylor don't," I shouted. "You'll only make it worse."

"I will not let him talk to you that way."

"And if you interfere, my life will only become worse. Please, let it go, I don't like it, but I can deal with it."

"This time, Carlie, but if it ever happens again, Willie and I are coming to blows."

"Good to know," Eddie shouted from where he was sitting in the corner. Taylor and I spun around and stared at him. The young scamp was grinning from ear to ear. Taylor started chuckling and was still snickering when he left the tent.

I gazed at the three-remaining people, Mai-Li's head was lowered, suddenly busy sorting through her medicine bag, Debbie waved, and Eddie grinned.

I took a deep breath, exhaled, and said. "Welcome home everybody, welcome home."

Chapter Seven

It took two days to haul the junk outside. Taylor discovered a creek flowing behind the outhouse which circled around the north side of the cabin. Mai-Li advised it was a run-off from the Tulameen River.

During the cleaning and hauling, there was no sign of Willie. Knowing Willie as we did, we knew he would return when he got hungry. By late afternoon, he shuffled out of the trees. Taylor was rummaging through the pile of garbage we removed from the cabin, salvaging pieces of wood and old nails that could be reused. Willie passed him without uttering a word and came and stood at the door. I was scrubbing the kitchen shelves and chose to ignore him. His constant hostile behaviour towards me was wearing on my nerves.

"You going to stand there all day holding up the wall, Willie?" Taylor inquired as he approached him. "Lots to be done."

Willie grumbled crossly, came inside, and shuffled through the pile of dust and dead leaves I swept to the middle of the room. Taylor gave him an annoyed look, and when I looked in his direction and shook my head, he let it ride. I grabbed an armload of empty wine bottles and beer cans and headed outside to the junk pile.

Taylor sensed my distress and grabbed Willie's arm to catch his attention and gestured towards the shed. "You can start in there, remove the trash, then scrub the floor and walls. Don't forget about the raccoon."

By the end of the day, the cabin and shed were empty, the dust and spider webs were swept away, and the walls and floors were scrubbed. Mai-Li spent the day caring for the kids, and they joined us inside. The cabin was comprised of one large room, and after much discussion, we decided we would sit on the floor to eat our meals. The boy's bedrolls would be set up on the west side of the cabin, and the girls on the east wall closer to the stove.

The attached shed could be entered through a door located on the west wall, and we discovered a second door in the shed that led outside to the outhouse. The shed would be perfect to store our wood supply, as well as our backpacks and weapons. Winters could be severe in the Cascade Mountains, and we needed to have a sizable supply of wood, if we were hit by a blizzard, we might be snowed in for weeks.

Mai-Li decided to put the water basin and bucket in the shed, and she reminded all of us to remove our muddy boots before coming inside the main room. She was busy enough without having to scrub muddy floors.

On the north wall was a counter with two cupboards underneath, and shelves above it. Mai-Li confiscated this space for the kitchen. The woodstove, repaired by Taylor and Willie, stood to the left of the cupboards. Thankfully, the squirrel and raccoon families were peacefully evicted, although I'm sure Eddie would have adopted them as pets if we let him.

I counted three windows, a prominent one in the front which offered an exposed view of the trees and bush and would alert us of any unwanted visitors, human or otherwise. A second window, found on the back wall, faced the backyard and the stream. A third smaller window, found on the east side above my sleeping bag, was missing two frames and Taylor salvaged wood from the junk pile which he nailed over the opening. For now, it worked, and when time permitted and before wintry weather arrived, he planned on sawing and shaping a plank he would nail over the two panes.

We dug through the pile of debris and salvaged as much of the furniture as possible. We found the remains of a wooden table, all four legs missing, which were more than likely used as firewood by passing drifters. Unfortunately, there were no chairs either. Taylor gathered as much of the wood as he could, and I assumed it would be added to the woodpile.

I watched in fascination as he emptied his backpack. He pulled out a saw, a hammer, a bag of nails, and an axe. When I peeked inside to find out what else he hoarded, he quickly fastened the flap, slapped my hand, and told me to mind my own business. I decided to make it a game and told the kids they could build whatever they wanted from the growing woodpile. Taylor frowned and did not respond. I decided he would eventually understand what I was doing, as Eddie needed to spend more time with him and Willie rather than being with Mai-Li, me, and Debbie all the time.

As Taylor predicted, the days turned bitter, we approached the end of November, and I noticed the worry lines on his face. The log cabin must be made livable, we needed wood, and our food supply was dwindling rapidly.

I heard Willie and Taylor discuss bagging a deer for the winter, and I knew Taylor was anxious the snow would arrive before they left.

The next morning, after we ate, I approached Taylor. "The wood is already cut into stove length, so I'll split them and pile them in the woodshed, and you guys can go hunting."

Taylor raised his eyebrows in disbelief, then solemnly refused my offer. I sighed, lifted the flap of the tent, and stepped outside. I trudged to the shed, retrieved the axe, sauntered over to the tree stump he intended to use as the base, grabbed a piece of wood and stood it on top. I raised my arms, swung the axe, and chopped it in half. I removed one of the halves, stood up the half that was left, then swung the axe again, turning it into a quarter piece. I repeated what I did four times, enjoying the astonished look on Taylor's face.

"Okay, you win," he chuckled, shaking his head. "How did you learn to do that?"

"From my dad, we had a wood-burning fireplace in our den, and it was something we did every Fall, filling the woodshed."

Taylor grinned, and I knew he would have kissed me if four nosey people weren't standing in front of the tent, watching our every move.

"Let's go, Willie," Taylor ordered. "Bring your rifle and leave your gun with the girls."

Willie started to reject, yet he shrewdly kept quiet when he spied the scowl on Taylor's face. They moved to the shed and finished packing, then headed across the yard and towards the treeline.

"We'll be back before dark," Taylor shouted as he turned and waved. "Eat without us. And tomorrow, Carlie, you start shooting lessons."

I began chopping wood, and commissioned Eddie and Debbie to haul the kindling into the shed and showed them how to pile them in stacks. Mai-Li moved the food supplies from the tent and stored them in the cupboards. While stopping for a light lunch, she took me aside and confessed she was troubled. She thought we had more food, and now with the berries gone, and the crackers almost finished, if the guys did not shoot a deer, we would be back to rationing. This concerned me, as four long months lay ahead of us.

Something was bothering me; this was not the first time I had this feeling. I hated it when this happened, it upset my stomach.

I worked through the morning and most of the afternoon. My arms were burning, and my back was warning me to stop. I decided to call it quits for the day and planned to finish the next morning.

Mai-Li spent most of the day moving things from the tent. I waylaid her and inquired about the kids.

"I haven't seen them in a while, I did hear them giggling. I presume they're in the shed, the doors have been closed most of the day. We better prepare ourselves."

I wandered inside the cabin and opened the shed door. Eddie and Debbie both froze.

"What is this?"

Silence.

"Okay, no one's speaking? This could earn both of you a time-out."

"No," Debbie wailed. "I don't like time-out."

By now Mai-Li heard the commotion and joined me inside. This time she did not interfere; she was letting me play this one on my own.

"I count maybe ten pieces of wood," I stated. "I've been splitting all day, what happened to the rest of them?"

"We borrowed them," Eddie mumbled.

"What did you do with them?"

He muttered a disjointed response, and I raised his chin and forced him to look directly at me.

"Eddie."

"We built a house, over by the outhouse."

Mai-Li and I opened the back door, then broke down, laughing until our sides hurt. When the kids realized they weren't in trouble, they jumped up and down, clapping their hands.

The wood was piled haphazardly in the shape of a square fort, with an opening in the front. A piece of coloured paper was nailed above the door, which was obviously a creation of Eddie's. The sign said, "WILLY'S HOUSE."

"Isn't it great Mai-Li, the kids made Willie a house."

"Yeah," Eddie mumbled. "That way he won't be mean to you anymore."

I sighed deeply, and realized it was time to have a word with this sensitive, caring boy. I did not want him worrying about Willie's behaviour towards me, it was my problem, and I somehow had to explain this to him.

"Eddie, come inside the cabin, please. Let's discuss Willie's house."

Remembering Mai-Li's cautions about the dwindling food supply, I gave the kids a cracker and a cup of water. Mai-Li joined Debbie on the far side of the room and played ball with her.

"Eddie, come sit beside me," I began. "Thank you so much for building Willie a house, it was a lot of work, although you should have asked him first to make sure it was okay. What if Willie doesn't want to be by himself and would prefer living with us."

"He says mean things to you, and that makes Taylor mad."

"Taylor gets angry sometimes because he wants all of us to get along."

Eddie leaned against my arm. "Taylor really likes you, that's why he doesn't want Willie to be mean to you."

I looked towards Mai-Li, who remained silent, no help from that corner.

Silence filled the room, and I decided it might be time to change the topic.

"Don't worry Eddie, I know it was a lot of work, but we'll have to take down Willie's house, okay?"

Eddie nodded, and I passed him the comics.

"Maybe Willie won't eat all our food," Debbie added nonchalantly as she rolled her ball back to Mai-Li.

I took a deep breath, again I was overcome with a sense of foreboding. I had no desire to take it any farther, yet I knew I had no choice. I looked at Mai-Li and she shrugged.

"He eats the same food we do Debbie," I said.

"Nu ah, he eats Mai-Li's berries, and the cookies, and lots of stuff."

Mai-Li set Debbie's ball on the floor then shuffled closer to her. "Debbie, how do you know Willie eats the food?"

"Cause I saw him. He gives me piggyback rides."

"That's right, he does, still you've only seen him take food a few times, right?"

Debbie picked up her ball and hugged it tightly to her chest, sensing the change in Mai-Li's tone.

Debbie scrunched her face, and I waited for the piercing scream.

"No crying," Mai-Li warned. "You're not in trouble, you just need to tell us what you saw."

"Will Willie be in trouble?"

"That depends on what you tell us."

Debbie looked at Eddie. He lowered his head and buried his face in my lap.

"I don't think he's been good," Debbie mumbled.

"Thank you, Debbie, you are a brave girl. Don't worry about it anymore." Mai-Li and I believed Debbie as she always told the truth, she did not understand the concept of lying.

"I'll tell you what," I suggested. "Why don't you and Eddie lay down and have a nap, and Mai-Li and I will stack the wood in the shed."

As soon as the kids were settled, we took Willie's house apart and hauled the wood inside. I was pleased to discover the shed was almost three-quarters full. By now, I was breathing heavily, and every muscle in my body ached.

Mai-Li and I checked on the kids, they were both sleeping. As soon as Taylor found out what Willie did, he would send him packing. Stealing food from your friends when they were struggling to survive, was heartless and an unforgivable offence.

Mai-Li and I decided we would wait until tomorrow before bringing up the matter. I did not look forward to the next day.

Chapter Eight

We spent the rest of the day keeping the kids occupied, then we ate a light supper. Later, I read to them, secretly wishing for new reading material. They didn't mind hearing the same thing over and over. They were soon fast asleep. Mai-Li and I did not mention the matter of the missing food, albeit we both knew it needed to be discussed and dealt with.

The daylight was almost gone, so we crept outside and started a campfire to wait for the guys return. Mai-Li brewed a pot of chicory. We stared into the flames, gripped by our personal thoughts.

We heard rustling in the bushes, and I picked up Willie's gun, which was lying on the ground next to me. Mai-Li reached down and removed her cane.

We spotted two dark silhouettes appearing from the trees, and I was relieved when I caught sight of Taylor. He raised his arm in greeting, and I set the gun on the ground.

Willie was clutching two grouse, and Taylor was empty-handed, apart from his weapons and backpack.

"Hello ladies," he mumbled wearily, as he and Willie approached the fire. Mai-Li handed him a cup of hot chicory, and he thanked her. Willie staggered towards the fire, dropped his gear, set the birds on the ground then reached for the mug Mai-Li handed to him.

"Taylor shot a buck," Willie volunteered. "And I bagged a couple of grouse."

"Wonderful," Mai-Li said cheerfully. "We're almost out of bear meat. Did you leave it close by?"

"A few kilometres back," Taylor answered. "We were just too bushed to lug it back. We spent the day climbing hills and scrambling over rocks. The deer is suspended in a cedar not far from here, the branch hangs over a cliff, so it should be safe from any passing carnivores. We'll go back and recover it tomorrow."

"You guys eaten yet?" I questioned, staring into the darkness, fearful my face might betray how I was feeling. I dared not look at Willie.

"Just what we packed this morning," Taylor replied. "A few crackers and this coffee should tide me over."

"I am sorry Taylor," Mai-Li replied. "The crackers are all gone."

"I thought we had a couple of bags left."

I gave Mai-Li a cursory glance, then turned and stared at the flickering flames. The four of us sat quietly. It was a cloudless night, the stars glittered brightly in the night sky. A wind blew across the yard, and I shivered. I could smell the snow and hoped we would be prepared when it arrived.

"Well, I'm exhausted enough to hit the sack," Willie muttered. "Hey, what did you guys do with the tent?"

"Mai-Li spent the day moving all the supplies into the cabin," I announced. "With the exception of a few items, she's almost finished."

"And most of the wood's been split," Taylor added, turning to look at the dwindling woodpile.

"The shed is three-quarters full, if you could cut a few more logs tomorrow, I'll finish while you salvage the meat. I wasn't sure where to store the axe, so I left it leaning against the wall."

Taylor nodded, then frowned when I gently pressed my palms face-down on my raised knees. He reached across and turned my hands over and inhaled sharply. My palms were covered with blisters.

Mai-Li frowned when she noticed them. "Carlie, why weren't you wearing your gloves?"

"I don't have any, just my mittens, the axe kept slipping, so I took them off."

"You should have told me; I have a salve that will relieve the pain and prevent infection?"

"Change of plans," Taylor spoke gruffly, looking directly at me. "Willie can finish the splitting tomorrow, and Carlie can come with me to recover the meat. I was going to start giving her lessons, but that'll have to wait until her hands are healed."

Willie, obviously upset with Taylor's decision, grabbed his backpack, and left. I doused the flames, then picked up his mug he left lying on the ground. Taylor grabbed his supplies and followed me, then stopped abruptly, shook his head angrily, and retrieved the grouse Willie draped earlier over a branch.

"I'll put them in the shed, they'll be okay until tomorrow, I'll have a talk with Willie and warn him about leaving animal carcasses around, the smell of the blood will be a calling card for anything lurking in the area."

I heard the frustration in Taylor's voice, and discreetly did not respond.

"Be quiet please," Mai-Li forewarned, as we approached the cabin. "Don't wake the kids."

"The place is looking amazing Mai-Li," Taylor whispered when he stepped inside. He moved noiselessly across the floor towards Willie, who was standing next to the shed door. He handed the birds to him. "Hang these on a nail, next time don't leave them outside." Then Taylor placed his backpack and weapons on the floor.

"Thanks for the loan of your gun," I told Willie when he returned to the main room.

"Wasn't my idea to leave it," he mumbled.

Mai-Li reached into the bottom cupboard and removed a leather pouch, motioning me to sit on my bedroll. Inside the pouch was a case crammed with pine needles; she took a damp cloth and wrapped it around the needles, making a poultice. Then she pressed it against my hand, instructing me to hold it securely.

"These are yew needles," she explained. "They are poisonous, if I use a slight amount in the poultice, it will be safe and will stop the pain and infection. Switch the poultice over to your left hand in ten minutes, return it to me, it must be burned; I don't want to chance the kids discovering it. In the morning, I will boil some willow bark and mix it in the bear fat, it makes a salve that is remarkable for blisters and burns."

Taylor was resting on his sleeping bag watching us. "Tomorrow we'll start using the wood stove, I want to check the fluepipe one last time, and I found a metal plate, where the pipe goes through, to protect the wall. I know the stove is placed in the centre of the room, but that's so the heat can reach into the corners, which we'll all appreciate once it turns cold. Unfortunately, seasoned wood burns best, so make sure the wood box is always full of dried wood."

"You sure know a lot about wood stoves," I said.

"As I've mentioned before, and before everything changed, Dad and I did a lot of camping and hunting and stayed in a cabin we owned that was heated by a wood stove. Now, I'm exhausted, and I'm calling it a night. Stay in your clothes tonight, it's going to be chilly in here. Night, ladies."

"Mai-Li turned to me and whispered. "Do you know where the bear skin is?"

"I put it in the shed; do you need it?"

"I think we should cover the kids with it, I can see my breath in here."

She tip-toed to the shed, grabbed the bearskin then spread it across the kids. I stared across the room, my thoughts racing. I was thankful we discovered the cabin; it was a haven for the winter, and we all needed a break from our strenuous journey.

I thought of Willie, we would let him finish cutting the wood, he owed us that much, and I was positive Mai-Li felt the same way. After supper and when the kids were in bed, we would have a lengthy conversation with Taylor. I was terrified what he would do, Willie broke the code, committing an unforgivable offence. For a second, I felt regret, then realized he would never change, he was lazy, selfish and a bully. I was almost positive Taylor would insist he leave the group. If that happened, we would be down to five in number, which would increase our workload. I would contribute as much as I could, I could chop wood, shovel snow, and learn to shoot so I could go hunting with Taylor. Mai-Li was happier watching the kids, cooking, and keeping things in order. I would also do the laundry even though it was a chore I loathed.

The next morning, we rolled up our bedrolls, and Mai-Li suggested we leave them in the corner next to the cupboard until we worked something out.

"I've been turning that over in my head," Taylor advised. "I'll build some shelves with the left-over wood and mount them in the shed and we can use them to store our backpacks and supplies. That should provide more room in here."

As he had mentioned the night before, Taylor double-checked the flue, then started a fire in the woodstove, and the room gradually warmed. Mai-Li made a pot of chicory, and I looked longingly at the kids' mugs filled with hot chocolate.

Mai-Li changed my poultices and instructed me to leave them on all day. She warned me not to do any of the meat cutting, as she feared I might pick up an infection. Otherwise, I was healthy, so carrying the venison would be no problem.

Willie stood quietly in the corner, scowling sullenly at being left behind. I walked past him on my way to the shed to get my jacket, toque, and mitts. I made sure my knife was in its sheath. I kissed the kids, warned them to behave and help Willie stack the rest of the wood in the shed after he finished chopping it, and lastly, not to build any more houses. Taylor was waiting for me outside, and I turned to look at the kids standing on the porch. Debbie blew me kisses, and I waved.

Taylor and I headed down the path, which was wide enough to stroll side by side. I enjoyed the bountiful trees, ferns and plants covering the forest bed. The sun shone through the dense branches, and I inhaled the scent of the sap and the pine needles. A squirrel chattered incessantly when we passed his nest which concealed his cache of seeds and nuts.

We spotted a doe standing behind a cedar. She watched us for a few seconds, more curious than afraid. Then she turned and disappeared into the forest.

"Too bad she wasn't around yesterday; it would have saved you and Willie a lot of hiking."

"I don't hunt nursing does," Taylor answered. "She probably has a fawn or is still training yearlings. With less hunters and people in the area, there are more bucks around, unfortunately they now know we are here, which is why we must broaden our hunting range to locate them."

Taylor stopped abruptly, and I bumped into him. He turned, then leaned over, and kissed me gently on my lips. I didn't move, and he removed his bow and rifle and set them on the ground, then he pulled me into his arms, and kissed me again, this time more passionately.

I put my arms around his neck and returned his kiss. My heart was pounding rapidly. Stunned, I pushed him away, stepped back, trying to catch my breath.

Taylor smiled, bent, and picked up his weapons. "Enough dillydallying," he whispered in my ear. "We have work to do."

Before I could defend myself, he leaned over and kissed me again, then pointed down the path. I was dazed, trying to piece together what just happened.

The trail disappeared and we struggled through heavy shrubs and bushes. The dried leaves fell noiselessly to the ground as we rubbed against them.

"Taylor," I hollered, stopping in the middle of the path. "That's a willow, we should mark this place for Mai-Li. She can use the bark and leaves to make her medicines and teas."

Taylor turned and walked back to join me by the tree. He examined it carefully. "It's healthy and the branches are perfect for making snowshoes, fish traps, baskets, rope, and more, things we'll need during the Winter. What a fabulous discovery Carlie."

"See," I teased. "I am useful for something."

"I know, I just found out. If we'd more time, I'd show you again."

My face flushed, and I stepped back angrily.

"Stop it."

"Does it bother you when I speak that way to you?" Taylor asked, looking directly at me.

"It embarrasses me."

"Why should you be embarrassed? You know how I feel about you, and I believe the way you reacted to my kiss, you feel the same about me."

"Maybe, a tiny bit," I whispered.

"What we share and do is private, it's nobody's business but our own."

"Not positive about that," I kidded. "I'll bet Eddie will know the minute we get back and walk through the door."

Taylor chuckled and shook his head. "You're probably right, he's much too perceptive for his age. Let's keep moving, we still have a bit of a stroll and a lot of work to do."

It took another half-hour before we were free of the underbrush. We paced across an open field and arrived at a ledge. I peeked over the side and spotted a winding river far below in the gorge.

"That's the Tulameen River, and as Mai-Li mentioned earlier, the brook flowing behind the cabin is a run-off," Taylor explained. "We should have flowing water all winter, which is probably why the original owner built where he did."

Eventually, we arrived at the treeline, and I looked around in dismay. Years back, an infestation of pine beetles destroyed hectares of trees, and with continuous climate changes and wildfires, the devastation was overwhelming.

Taylor placed his arm around my waist. "I know, it's distressing, so much of our timber has disappeared, and it will take hundreds of years to grow back. At first, the logging companies planted new shoots to replace the trees they felled, which worked for a while. With the extreme climate changes the new growth was destroyed by wildfires, which were started by nature, or far too often, by irresponsible, thoughtless people."

"How do you know all this stuff?" I asked.

"My Dad taught me about nature, animals, and tracking, information he felt I needed to know to survive in the wilderness. He even taught me how to read the stars."

"Almost as if he knew you would need it one day," I whispered.

Taylor looked at me for the longest time. Then he reached over and took my hand. "The rest I learned from reading. My nose was always in a book, didn't matter what it was about, I read it."

I chuckled. "Can't picture you as a bookworm, I can however picture you as a jock."

"Did that too. I competed in all kinds of sports, hockey, baseball, swimming, and track and field. How about you?"

I turned my head. "I read a lot too, my parents instilled that in me. They both attended university, all the way, we had a den and library in our house. I was expected to do well in school. Then I became a dreaded teenager and spent all my time on my computer or iPad, locked in my bedroom. I was awful, so moody and angry all the time. I frustrated them a lot, they probably thought I was destined for the streets.”

“Spoiled little rich girl.”

“We weren’t rich.”

“You grew up in a spacious house on Marine Drive, a few blocks from the Pacific Ocean. Both your parents were seismologists, working for the University. However, regardless of how wealthy your parents were, Carlie, they both loved you unconditionally.”

“Well, I fulfilled one of their predictions. I did end up on the streets.”

“Come on, we can reminisce later, we’re just about there.”

I spotted a huge cedar growing a few centimetres away from an embankment. Some of the boughs hung over the edge and I noticed a deer trussed securely to the limb.

Taylor paced around the tree, then gestured me to join him. I noticed tracks on the ground and bent down to study them. “Wow, bear tracks, and they’re recent.”

“Good job Carlie.”

“Thank you, thank you.”

“How did you learn to read tracks?”

“From you. Every time we spotted footprints, you would announce. ‘Bear tracks, and they’re fresh.’”

Taylor grabbed me and tickled me and I shrieked and told him to stop. I punched his arm, his eyes widened, then he kissed my neck and my lips. "Regretfully," he whispered. "I haven't got time for anything else, maybe later."

I stood unmoving and watched him take a coil of rope from his backpack, then throw it over the hanging branch.

"Okay, I need you to pull the rope when I untie the deer. Carlie, are you listening to me?"

I raised my head and stared at him. Disoriented, I shook my head, then took the end of the rope from him. He climbed the tree, using the limbs as footholds. When he reached the overhanging bough, he lay on his stomach and then shimmied over to the deer, untying the ropes.

"Keep your hands protected. Put on your mittens. When we get back, I'll ask Mai-Li to make you gloves, should be some deer hide left."

I nodded, then shuffled warily to the edge of the ridge.

Don't look down, don't look down.

"Now grab the rope and pull as hard as you can, and don't let go."

I wound the rope around my shoulder and pulled backwards. Taylor lowered the deer, and when it was a few centimetres above my head, I grabbed it and let it fall to the ground.

"Thanks, always great to have a second pair of hands, by the way, how are they?"

Startled, I turned and faced him. I hadn't heard a sound when he jumped out of the tree. I hated when he did that.

"Um fine, Mai-Li makes a wicked poultice."

Taylor took out a saw and a knife from his pack.

Something was bothering me, and I couldn't quite place it. I looked at the branch, then down at the deer.

"You okay, you're not queasy about butchering the deer; you have a weird look on your face."

"You jerk," I yelled.

"Whoa," he reacted, raising his hands in defence.

"The whole rope thing was bogus. You just threw it over the branch, you didn't need it at all to lower the deer. You made me pull the stupid thing for nothing. I must have looked like an idiot."

Taylor laughed. I looked away, more embarrassed than angry.

"Aw, come on Carlie. I was just teasing you. Besides, we need something different to chat about at the supper table."

"Oh, we will, sooner than you realize."

Taylor's smile left his face. "Now you're scaring me."

"About time," I muttered.

Then I removed the gunny sacks from my backpack; Taylor stared at me, shrugged, then began carving the deer.

Chapter Nine

Harvesting the deer was a tedious, revolting process; we salvaged as much as we could. Our packs were heavy, and we stopped often to rest, more for my sake than Taylor's. We arrived back at the cabin late in the afternoon.

The kids noticed us coming and rushed towards us. I warned them to stay back as we were covered in blood. Debbie scrunched her face. I heard Mai-Li giggling as she stood behind her.

Eddie's greeting was quite different. His face lit up, and he gazed at Taylor as if he was a hero. "Cool," he uttered, then gave Taylor a high five.

"Hey," I stammered. "What about me?"

Looking in my direction, he joked. "Good job Carlie."

I inhaled sharply, he looked so much like Rusty, I fought back tears. Taylor noticed my reaction and came and stood behind me.

"Let's put these packs down," he whispered. "They're not getting any lighter."

I nodded, then looked around the yard. The pile of lumber was gone and so was Willie.

"Shush," Eddie warned, pursing his lips. "We gotta be quiet; we don't want to wake up Willie. He was really busy today."

I rolled my eyes, Taylor grinned, then bent over and ruffled Eddie's hair. I trudged behind him towards the back door and entered the shed. We removed our packs and hung them on the pegs. "We'll leave them here; it should be cold enough tonight to keep the meat until tomorrow. Let's wash up."

I removed the metal wash basin and scrub brush from the wall. A small bag hung on the same hook; I looked inside and found the remains of our precious hand soap.

I trailed Taylor to the creek, filled the basin, and rubbed some of the soap on the brush. I scrubbed my arms, neck, and face, then I handed everything to Taylor and told him when he was finished to give me his clothes.

"Finally," he spoke, grinning from ear to ear.

I should have known better.

I clenched my teeth, in no mood to be joking around. "When you change your clothes after we get back inside, give them to me. I'm doing laundry tomorrow. And take your mind out of the gutter. You need to behave around the others, or have you forgotten everything we discussed."

"Mai-Li and the kids will just laugh. It's not as if they don't know how I feel about you."

"I wasn't talking about them; I was referring to Willie." I turned my head and slowly stood.

"How come when Willie's name comes up, you get an uneasy look on your face? Has he been harassing you again?"

"No more than usual, nothing I can't manage."

"Well, I'm going to be around a lot more, and if he tries anything, I'll set him straight. He needs to learn what his boundaries are."

"You mean like the ones you cross?" I implied.

Taylor stood, a tight-lipped smile crossing his face. "If you're uncomfortable with my advances, then I'll stop."

I stepped back, shocked by his outrage. Taylor reached over and gripped my hands. "Carlie, I'm sorry, I didn't mean to sound so harsh. You know I fell in love with you the moment we met."

I felt my face redden, I stared at the ground, not knowing how to answer.

"Carlie, I'll always protect you, and whether you know it or not, you care about me too."

"I don't know if I do, all I feel right now is sadness, I'm still mourning Rusty, and I'm not ready to move forward. I enjoy when we kiss and when you hold me, but right now, I don't want to take it any farther."

"I understand how you feel, and I'll honour your wishes, but you need to know being near you all the time makes it hard not to touch you.”

I lifted my head and stared into his eyes. “I know, I sometimes feel that way about you too.”

Taylor kissed me tenderly and whispered. “Good to know.”

Crap, he knows how flustered I get when he says that.

I slapped his arm. “Come on, let’s go back inside.” I pointed towards the cabin. “We have a captive audience.”

Three smiling faces at the window watched as we marched up the hill.

By the time we got inside, Mai-Li was at the stove. She poured each of us a cup of hot chicory. I tried to show my appreciation with everything she did for us, but I so wanted a cup of real coffee.

Willie was in the far corner snoring loudly. I looked at Mai-Li and she lowered her head. “Hope you guys are hungry,” she bragged. “I cooked stuffed grouse for supper.”

“Wow sounds delicious. Can I give you a hand?” I offered.

“No, you’ve worked enough today. Go sit on the porch and relax.”

Taylor and I strolled outside, pursued by two enthusiastic kids.

“You two leave them alone,” Mai-Li shouted after them.

“It’s okay Mai-Li, we haven’t seen them all day,” Taylor replied.

The kids squeezed themselves between us, Debbie next to me and Eddie leaning against Taylor's leg. They babbled at the same time, and soon my head was spinning trying to catch both conversations. I took tiny sips of the chicory and Taylor leaned back on the step, thoroughly enjoying the kids.

He'll make a wonderful father one day.

What, where did that come from? And right after I just spoke to him about backing off. Jeez a couple of kisses, and I was ready to have kids with the guy. What was wrong with me?

Taylor finished his coffee and set his mug on the step. "Who wants to play ball?"

Two eager kids raced into the yard, I placed my almost full cup of chicory on the porch and chased after them.

"Would you care to finish your chicory?" Taylor asked as I raced past him. "Or do you want me to wait while you pour it in the bushes?"

"You rat on me to Mai-Li and you're dead meat."

He grinned, then grabbed Debbie's ball. Soon we were in the middle of a noisy rambunctious game of throw the ball, scurry after the ball, catch the ball, and persuade Debbie to share the ball.

We kept the kids entertained for another half hour, as my hands were still sore, I spent more time chasing the ball than catching it. I finally called the game to a halt. "Okay, it's late, let's go inside and you can read comics and colour."

After confiscating the comics from Willie's bag, the kids settled down. The heat from the woodstove was comforting, and Mai-Li and I set out the dishes and cutlery on our makeshift table on the floor.

"Suppers ready," Mai-Li informed us. "Debbie, why don't you wake up Willie."

Debbie raced over to him and shook his arm. "Willie, suppers ready."

It didn't take him long to join us on the floor.

"Eddie, Debbie," Mai-Li warned, "Wait until the food cools or you'll burn your tongues."

The plates were licked clean. Mai-Li removed a bag from the cupboard and handed around chocolate chip cookies.

We were told all the cookies were gone, as we stared at her in surprise. "I was saving these for a rainy day," she muttered.

"Mai-Li, it's not raining, "Eddie giggled.

"I know, I got tired of waiting."

We all laughed, I looked at Mai-Li as she turned away. More than ever, I dreaded what was to come.

Soon it was time to put the kids to bed. They washed their faces, then chewed willow bark to clean their teeth. Mai-Li swore if we used it daily, we would not get cavities. The last thing we needed would be for one of the kids to get a toothache.

"Okay, into your PJ'S," I ordered.

"No, it's too cold," Debbie lamented.

"From now on, we're going to keep the fire going at night," Taylor interrupted. "It'll be cozy and comfortable; we have no shortage of wood."

The kids were soon tucked in, and the bearskin was thrown across them. I asked what they wanted me to read, surprisingly, they both wanted a story. Not that I blamed them, they probably knew all the comics by heart. As was the procedure, they were both dead to the world before I got to the best part.

I realized the time had come. My hands were shaking, I took a shallow breath, and nervously bit my nails. I looked at Mai-Li and she nodded. We discussed it earlier as to how we would broach the topic, and it was decided she would be the one to start.

"If I could, I want to discuss a matter that has come up," she began. Taylor and Willie looked at her.

"When I was checking the food supply, I discovered not only my berries, but there was a lot more missing."

Taylor frowned then straightened up. "What's missing?"

"Two boxes of crackers, three cans of peaches, and a considerable portion of the bear meat."

"That's extremely serious, Mai-Li, did we drop a bag somewhere on the trail."

"No, I don't think so. They were all accounted for when we got here. I keep a close tab of everything."

"I know you do. How low are we? Do we have enough to make it through the winter?"

"If you hadn't shot the deer, we would have been back on rationing. As it is, it's going to be tough going."

"Willie, do you have anything to say, you're awfully quiet," Taylor inquired, turning to face him.

"What the hell, are you blaming me?"

"Keep your voice down, we just got the kids to sleep. When you're quiet, I get nervous. Just answer my question."

"I have nothing to say."

"I do," I acknowledged, looking at Willie. "Just let me finish before you interrupt. When you were out hunting, Mai-Li and I discussed the missing food. The kids were listening, Debbie told us she saw you take berries, crackers, and other foodstuff."

"Debbie," Willie scoffed. "She's hardly a reliable source, now, is she?"

I inhaled angrily. "At first, just so you know, when we questioned her, she didn't answer; she's fond of you and considers you her friend."

"That's her problem."

I shook my head in revulsion, at times, Willie was cruel and thoughtless, focusing utterly on himself. Any chores he did were done reluctantly, and if he weren't so petrified of Taylor, our existences would have been unbearable.

"When we questioned Debbie again, she looked at Eddie, and we knew by the looks on their faces she wasn't lying, she doesn't know how."

"Bullshit, and you know it, bitch. You'd say anything to get me in trouble. Ever since we first met, you've been on my case. I know the only reason you let me stay at the warehouse at Little Mountain was because I knew where the food supply was buried, and you needed me. You've never accepted me as a friend or part of the gang."

Before anyone realized what had happened, Taylor jumped up and wrenched Willie out of his bedroll. He wrapped his arm around his throat. I started to rise, and Mai-Li reached over and restrained me.

"You never learn, do you, Willie," Taylor growled, clenching his teeth, his face rigid with anger, and I realized he was strong enough to harm Willie if he had an inclination to do so.

Willie knew enough to keep quiet; he bit his lip, and drops of perspiration dotted his forehead.

No one moved for the longest time. Taylor released his hold and shoved Willie back down. Willie's face was red with anger, he reached inside his bag, and I realized at once what he planned to do. I jumped up and stomped on his hand forcefully. He yowled, cursing and moaning.

"You try that again, and I swear I'll hit you with the frying pan," I threatened.

Taylor reached over and threw back the edge of the sleeping bag. Willie's gun was lying on the floor. Taylor turned and looked at me, then gestured for me to move back. I fled to the far side of the room and sat next to Mai-Li.

"What did you plan on doing with this?" he glared, pointing to the gun.

"You figure it out, you're so smart," Willie spat, holding his injured hand firmly against his chest.

"You have ten minutes to retrieve your gear, and to get the hell out of here. I don't want to see your face again; do I make myself clear?"

Willie stood in wide-eyed shock, then shook his head in disbelief. "You can't do that, it's the middle of the night, it's freezing outside."

"Not my problem, you brought this on yourself. Because of your greed and disregard, you left five people with barely enough food to make it through the winter. You broke the code Willie, and you're lucky to receive just a bruised hand."

"What code, this is hardly a gang. It's a bunch of misfits."

"This bunch of misfits has more integrity than any gang I've ever belonged to or come across. You belong back at Little Mountain, or with the Desert Rats, it's your choice, take your pick."

"Both of them would be glad to welcome me back."

"It's not what I heard on the streets at Little Mountain. Before you arrived at the warehouse, you were kicked out of your gang for stealing food?"

Willie did not defend himself, he stood and stared angrily at the far wall. Taylor went to the shed and retrieved Willie's backpack, hip flask, and coat. He returned and threw them on the floor. A box of crackers, two tins of peaches, granola bars, and chocolate packets landed on the floor.

"That's mine," Willie yelled, bending to grab the food. Taylor restrained him, grasped his arm, and pulled it behind his back. Willie twisted angrily, and Taylor released his hold.

"Your ten minutes are up," he threatened, without taking his gaze off Willie.

Willie knew he didn't stand a chance against Taylor. He struggled into his coat, then grabbed his bedroll and backpack. "I have to get my weapons and ammo," he muttered, heading towards the woodshed.

Taylor stopped him with his arm, shook his head, and pointed towards the front door.

"The rifle, I believe is mine. I put your gun and a few rounds of ammunition in your pack, don't waste it; there's no shortage of wild animals prowling around, especially in the middle of the night."

"Where am I supposed to go?"

"I don't really care, you can return to Vancouver, but I don't consider that a smart move on your part. Maybe try the Desert Rats."

"It's going to start snowing any day and you know it. You're as good as killing me."

"Then I guess we're even."

Taylor opened the door and waited until Willie stepped outside.

"Keep your head up West, I'll be back for you."

"Don't try it, Willie."

"Then maybe I'll come back for someone you care about."

Taylor's back stiffened, he did not respond to Willie's threat.

We watched as Willie staggered down the steps, then headed into the bush. Taylor quietly shut the door. "I'm not surprised, for a while, I thought he had changed, that he'd matured a bit. Guess I was wrong."

"You can't blame yourself," Mai-Li pondered. "Willie is a lost soul, maybe one day he will discover peace."

I was exhausted, and the strain must have shown on my face. Taylor kissed me, then whispered. "Don't let his threat trouble you, he's gone, he won't bother you again."

Then Taylor strolled to his overnight bag. He removed his gun from inside his shirt and placed it on the floor. He must have taken it from his pack when he retrieved Willie's equipment.

Mai-Li and I went to the shed and dressed in our PJs. We returned to the main room; Taylor's back was turned away from us; I knew he was outraged with Willie and was trying to process what just happened.

Mai-Li shut off the flashlight and the cabin was in darkness.

I wrapped my sleeping bag tightly around my body and closed my eyes. I tossed for hours, and eventually fell into a restless sleep.

Chapter Ten

The next morning, we drank our chicory in silence. Eddie and Debbie woke, pulled on their boots, and raced outside to the outdoor toilet.

Mai-Li started breakfast, and I put out clean clothes for the kids. It wasn't long before we heard them giggling in the shed. A full bucket of water was left next to the washbasin, and they were expected to wash their hands after using the outhouse.

I drifted to the shed and watched Eddie pour water into the basin. I loaded my arms with kindling and wood, and returned to the kitchen, and stacked it in the wood box next to the stove. I returned for a second load and grinned when I watched Debbie lean over the basin. Eddie poured water over her head, and it flowed down her back and splashed on the floor. When he did it a second time, I figured it was time to shut down the waterworks.

"Eddie, not so much water, Debbie's PJs are soaked."

"It's okay, Carlie," Debbie replied, lifting her head, spraying water everywhere.

"I'm teaching her to swim," Eddie said.

"That's enough swimming lessons for one day. I'll have to wipe this mess up, so vamoose inside and put on some dry clothes. Debbie, here's a towel."

The door opened, Taylor entered as I bent over and struggled to wrap the towel around Debbie's head. Eddie was startled and dropped the ladle full of water, it splashed down my face, covering my shirt and jeans.

"Eddie," I squealed in shock.

"Oops sorry, Carlie," he said. "Are you okay?"

"I'm fine Eddie, just put on some dry clothes," I replied in frustration. "And don't forget to take Debbie with you."

I heard laughter and spun around angrily. Taylor's smile disappeared, and he quietly slipped past me and left by the back door. I stuffed my arms with wood and pushed the cabin door open with my shoulder. We did not burn any wood during the day, as most of the time, we were outside. Mai-Li started the stove half an hour before supper, and we kept it on during the night. For now, it worked; once the weather got worse, we would spend more time indoors. Keeping the wood box full would be an ongoing chore. Losing Willie made more work for all of us.

Mai-Li rubbed Debbie's wet hair with the towel, while the young girl screamed and fought to escape. She heard my movements and turned to face me. One look at my face, my dripping hair, and my clothes, was enough for her to remain quiet.

I dug through my pack, pulled out dry clothes, and hurried back to the shed to change. I removed my bra and T-shirt when the side door suddenly opened. I quickly lifted my shirt to cover myself. Taylor grinned and I waited for him to make a clever remark, then waited impatiently for him to leave. As he passed me on his way to the cabin, he turned, lowered his head, and whispered in my ear. "If we were alone, it would have taken you a lot longer to get dressed."

My face burned red, and I stared at his retreating back. I quickly dressed and wrapped my wet clothing in a bundle and joined the others. Mai-Li filled the plates and handed one to me.

"You okay Carlie, your face is flushed. You're not catching something, are you?"

I shook my head and sat in my usual place on the floor. I picked up my fork and took a bite, finding it awkward to swallow. I could feel Taylor watching me.

"We better call Willie." Debbie said, suddenly noticing one less person in our group.

"He never misses eating," Eddie commented.

Mai-Li and I looked at Taylor. He laid his plate on the floor. "I have something to tell you. Willie has left, he won't be coming back."

Eddie was quiet for the longest time. "I know why he's gone; he was mean to Carlie."

"He was, it's one of the reasons we asked him to leave, just not the main one."

"Na ah Eddie," Debbie added. "It's cause he stole our food, and now we might die cause we'll starve to death."

We all started speaking at once. Taylor raised his hand, and we quieted down. "Debbie, Eddie, we won't lie to you, he did steal our food, which is a terrible thing to do. And no, we will not die of starvation, I'll make sure we don't."

The kids nodded, then picked up their plates and continued eating, comfortable with Taylor's explanation. I was surprised they did not ask more about Willie being asked to leave. They were both young, yet understood the reason Willie was gone, they both seemed aware of the severity of his actions.

"I've salvaged some of the old wood," Taylor declared, changing the topic. "We have enough to make wooden pegs and shelves. I'll put the pegs in the shed to hang our coats and store the meat that needs to be kept cold. Then I'll place a few of the shelves above the pegs to keep our bags and the bear skin, and the rest of the shelves I'll put in the kitchen to store clothes and kid's toys. How does that sound?"

Eddie and Debbie nodded; they were too occupied eating to get excited. I realized Taylor mentioned the topic as he didn't want to answer any further embarrassing questions about Willie's disappearance. Surprisingly, Debbie took it better than we thought.

Taylor decided to change his tactic. "I was hoping you could lend a hand, Eddie. I need help with the sawing and hammering, it's okay if you can't. I can ask Carlie."

Eddie sighed heavily, stood, and moved towards Taylor. He put his hand on Taylor's shoulder, leaned over and whispered. "I better do it, Carlie's not so great building stuff."

"Hey," I countered. "I'm right here."

"Before we pass judgment, Eddie," Taylor replied, in a serious voice. "What evidence do you have?"

"You should have seen what she did at the warehouse."

"Oh, oh, should I listen to this?" Taylor replied.

Eddie nodded wisely. "The cupboard door in the kitchen, remember the one with the rope keeping it shut."

"No, she didn't?"

"She did, she did," Debbie squealed, jumping up and down.

"Etui, Debbie," I muttered.

"Well, if that's all she did wrong, that's not so bad," Taylor reasoned.

"Wait, I have more," Eddie added. "Lots more."

"I apologize, Carlie," Taylor declared, looking my way "Better than having the shelves fall on someone's head."

"Not fair," I remarked. "And you're having far too much fun at my expense."

"Your day in court will come," Taylor grinned. "Eddie, it's your move."

Eddie frowned, uncertain of what Taylor meant.

"Go ahead, guy," Taylor uttered.

"It's about the toilet."

I almost told him to stop, although I would probably have been thrown out for contempt. Mai-Li smiled, enjoying herself immensely.

"The toilet and the lid were broken to pieces; it was really stinky," Eddie revealed, making a disgusted face.

"Go on, keep going," Taylor encouraged.

"She found a rusty pail, and we had to use it as the toilet, and then she found a frying pan, and that was the lid."

Taylor shook his head in dismay then thought a moment before answering. "It all comes back now, Eddie; say no more, you're hired."

"Hurrah," Eddie cried, doing a jig. Debbie, of course, cheered him on.

Realizing the trial was over, and a verdict passed, I decided to move on to other matters. Secretly, I was pleased Taylor was including the kids as Eddie was never happier when he was with Taylor learning something new, and Debbie shadowed her friend faithfully.

"Since Taylor and Eddie are in charge of the carpentry, they can start now," I exclaimed interrupting the frivolity. "I have a shed floor to mop, and I planned on airing the sleeping bags today."

"Come on kids, let's go outside," Taylor began. "I've hauled a pile of discarded wood to the back yard. We can start right away."

"Whoa, whoa," I yelled. "Put on your coats and mittens first, which means you too Taylor."

Taylor raced across the floor and opened the shed door. "Last one out is a rotten egg."

The kids squealed in excitement, chasing after him.

"Watch out, those floors are slippery," I warned.

Boom!

Eddie and Debbie burst out laughing, and I heard Taylor cursing angrily. "I'm covered in mud," he bellowed.

"It'll wash out. Mai-Li and I are doing laundry tomorrow, you can give us a hand."

"Don't count on it," he snapped. "Come on kids, I'm not getting any sympathy here."

We watched from the side window as he and the kids raced down the incline behind the cabin. Before we started moving our provisions inside, Taylor hastily assembled a shed at the bottom of the hill, telling us he wanted to use it as a workshop. At the time, I thought it was a waste of energy and time, now I understood his reasoning. He was extremely organized and always one step ahead of the rest of us.

"I hope the kids behave and not slow Taylor down," Mai-Li muttered. "He has a lot of work to get done."

"He'll be fine, he's the one who invited them, besides, it's wonderful practice."

"For what?"

"I don't know if you've noticed, he's a bit impatient when it comes to the kids."

"Well, we all have our shortcomings."

"Except you, Mai-Li, I've never heard you lose your temper, you are so tolerant."

"Thank you, Carlie, I must confess, there were times I longed to whack my cane over Willie's head. The kids can be a handful, I even threatened them once."

"So, I threaten them all the time," I replied.

"I know, but they know you don't mean it."

"Hey, wait a minute...yeah, you're right."

Mai-Li sighed. "Yet I can't envisage being without them, they bring so much joy to our group."

I inhaled sharply, and Mai-Li reached over and covered my hand. "We all miss him, Carlie."

"At times I hurt so much I can't breathe."

"We all mourn in different ways, Eddie told us Rusty is happy, and I believe him, don't you?"

"That's another thing that makes me uncomfortable. Do you think it's his way of coping with this whole thing?"

"No, I imagine he did that a long time ago, he shared a special bond with Rusty."

Not wanting to pursue the topic, I stepped away from the window. "Time to start cleaning. Do you have a list of the food we have left?"

"Yes, I do, and even what Taylor recovered from Willie's stash, we are still low on provisions. I hope to gather as many herbs, berries, and roots as I can before the weather turns. Can you help me?"

"Of course, let's do that tomorrow, Taylor won't mind smoking the deer meat, we can relieve him when we return. The clothes can wait for another day."

"Anything from getting out of doing laundry," Mai-Li whispered as she turned away.

I sniggered half-heartedly and went to the woodshed to survey the damage and almost cried. Water spattered up the walls, mud caked the floor, and I glanced at the skid mark Taylor made when he fell.

"Water's hot," Mai-Li said.

I returned with a bucket and filled it with water. I found the box of laundry soap and stirred in a small piece. Mai-Li found our scrub brush buried in the kitchen supplies. We had confiscated an old broom left in the cabin; I started sweeping, and the dried mud and dirt rose in a murky cloud, making me cough. I opened the back door and swept the debris outside.

"Before you start scrubbing, protect your hands," Mai-Li called from the kitchen.

"I don't have anything to put on them. Can you make another poultice?"

"No," she responded, as she entered the room. "I'm out of yew needles. I have a few pieces of bear hide. Let me wrap your hands with that."

Once my hands were covered, I started scrubbing; I was ready to throttle Eddie and Debbie. Then I recalled my talk with Mai-Li about Taylor being impatient, and decided now was a fitting time for me to start working on my own faults.

After I finished scrubbing the shed, I hauled the sleeping bags outside and spread them across the bushes to air.

It was mid-morning, and as I finished earlier than expected, I decided to start smoking the deer meat. Taylor could work on it tomorrow while Mai-Li and I went scavenging.

I gathered tinder, dried moss, twigs, leaves, and needles for kindling. Fallen branches and leftover wood covered the ground and worked well as fuel. I started a pile next to the chopping block, the most open spot in the yard and near enough to run for cover in the event unexpected guests arrived at our door.

We had a limited supply of matches Mai-Li sometimes used to start the wood stove.

She made a point of keeping the embers stoked, as the matches were to be used only for emergencies.

I recalled reading a camping book years ago on how to start a fire by rubbing two dried sticks rapidly together, probably something I learned from my disastrous attempt at being a Girl Guide. It didn't take my parents long to realize I was happier taking swimming lessons or drawing and painting.

Twenty minutes later, my back and arms burning, I admitted defeat. I wandered around to the back and headed down the slope towards the sound of laughter. Taylor was sawing a piece of wood, Eddie pounded nails and Debbie crawled around on her knees gathering sawdust and wood chips.

Taylor stopped sawing when he caught sight of me. "Hi, you ladies keeping yourselves busy?"

"The woodshed is clean and free of mud, and the bags are being aired. I've been collecting firewood to start a fire as I thought I'd start smoking the deer meat."

"Crap, the deer, I forgot," Taylor groaned, running his fingers through his hair. "I'll join you in a minute."

"No, it's all right. Mai-Li and I can keep an eye on it. But I'm having trouble starting the fire."

"What's wrong?"

"I know the matches have to be used sparingly, so I rubbed two sticks together, but it didn't work."

Eddie, standing next to Taylor, smacked the top of his forehead, and Debbie copied his gesture. "Carlie, you can't start a fire with sticks."

Taylor lowered his head, a grin creasing his face. "I have a flint and steel kit. Come on, I'll get it and show you how to use it."

He noticed the bear skin covering my hands and shook his head. "Rubbing two sticks together to start a fire is a skill that takes many years to learn, and I suppose your hands are throbbing by now. You're right about the matches; they're only to be used in an emergency."

"The morning is just about gone, we might as well have lunch now before I start," I suggested.

When we arrived at the back door of the shed, I made Taylor and the kids remove their boots. I was shocked to discover Eddie's were worn to the insole. Another worry to add to my list. I wondered if Mai-Li knew how to make moccasins from deer hide.

We took off our coats and threw them on the woodpile. Debbie's mitts were missing, and Eddie pulled them from his pocket and laid them beside his.

Mai-Li's face was flushed from standing over the stove. "Right on time," she advised.

"I'm heating the last of the bear stew. Wash up, please."

"I moved the basin and soap in here," I spoke up. "It's in the corner for now, we'll need to find a better place. And no more water fights."

Eddie's face blushed red with embarrassment. He took Debbie's hand, and they sat on the floor.

Mai-Li spooned the stew into mugs and warned the kids it was hot. Debbie immediately took a spoonful and screamed. Mai-Li serenely handed her a cup of water and peace was restored.

"There's been a change of plans," I told Taylor. "Mai-Li is bent on replenishing her herbs, berries, and plants before it snows. She and I are going to do that tomorrow, so the laundry can wait another day. Two things, Taylor: Can you finish smoking the deer meat, and can you babysit the kids while we are gone."

"We're not babies," Eddie proclaimed indignantly. "It's okay Taylor, you don't have to babysit us. Right, Debbie."

"Right, we're not babies, "Debbie piped in.

"Then I guess you only have one thing to worry about," I assured Taylor.

After lunch was over, Taylor showed me how to start the fire using flint and steel. He returned to his workshop; the kids ran to keep up with him.

The first thing I did was make a miniature teepee out of three tree branches stripped and chopped down to the same size, which I tied with willow strips. I then cut and stripped three shorter branches and tied them horizontally around the sides of the teepee. To finish off, I collected thicker boughs and laid them a few centimetres apart, forming a platform to smoke the meat by laying it down or hanging it between the spaces. I stuffed the kindling under the platform and waited for the wood to start burning.

Since leaving the Wastelands, Mai-Li never passed a willow without collecting its stems. I questioned her why she wanted so many, and she told me she could make several things from them. I suddenly remembered the willow Taylor and I passed on our way to retrieve the deer. I mentioned it to Mai-Li, and she suggested we look at it tomorrow.

She joined me outside and cut the fat and silver skin from the meat. No way was I going to ask her how she prepared them to make her medicines or salves.

We laid and hung the strips of meat on the platform, then we took Taylor's tarp and wrapped it around the teepee to keep the smoke inside. I was amazed that it worked.

We sat cross-legged on the ground and kept an eye on the meat. Mai-Li presented the list of food supplies left and even with the food recovered by Taylor, I was shocked to learn how much Willie ate before he was discovered.

"Why do you suppose he did that?" I asked.

"Willie doesn't do it to be mean or vindictive, he eats for comfort. We all have our ways of coping, and this is his. Being ousted from the group by Taylor is an enormous upset for him, but we had no other alternative. If we plan to reach our destination, we must pull our weight. The children are our priority."

"I agree, and I expect Willie's treatment towards me might have been a part of the reason Taylor kicked him out."

Mai-Li nodded perceptively. "It has been an issue from the onset, and animosity between two people the entire group relies so heavily on is not beneficial. Emotions can create havoc if they are allowed to fester, Taylor had no choice."

"I never encouraged Willie in any way, still he egged me on even when he knows it irritates Taylor. Willie has no feelings for me, he has a different attitude towards women, specifically in the way he treats them."

"That's partially true, Carlie. His upbringing was hard, and he did not get a lot of affection in his life."

I looked at Mai-Li in surprise. "Did you know Willie before the earthquake?"

"No, we communicated during our travels. His father was a fisherman, earning insufficient money to feed his family. Many times, Willie went to bed hungry. His mother he never knew, she left Willie and his father when he was young, which is probably why he treats women the way he does."

"I didn't know that, but it still doesn't mean he can treat me the way he does, or when he belittles Debbie because of her disability."

Mai-Li shook her head despondently. "Ever since the firestorm, Willie struggled with his emotions regarding Debbie, as she openly received him as her friend."

"I've noticed that as well. Yet his attitude towards me never changed, I suppose I irritate him as our personalities are so different, we can't all be close friends."

Mai-Li raised her head and stared at the trees, then turned and looked at me. "Carlie, Willie has feelings for you too, he's jealous as Taylor pursued you from the moment he joined the Rug Rats. I realize you have never encouraged or indicated to Willie you cared for him. I hope he finds a place where he will be received and eventually find peace."

I thought a moment before answering. "I guess we all deserve to be happy, perhaps being away from us is what Willie needs."

"True," Mai-Li replied solemnly. "Now, about tomorrow. Let's check my list to make sure I haven't missed anything."

She reached inside her pocket, removed one of the coloured papers the kids used for their drawing, then opened it. She had itemized the names of the plants, dried berries, and herbs, as well as a willow she planned to look for. It was getting late in the year to gather most of the samples, yet she hoped to collect enough to replenish her supplies.

Hours passed, and I told Mai-Li I was going to check on the kids. She was weaving a basket and told me she planned to make a hide scraper once the basket was finished. I heard her and Taylor talking earlier about making a fish trap and maybe snowshoes. I often wondered how our lives would have been if we didn't have Taylor and Mai-Li's creative talents.

I traipsed down the hill towards the woodshop and watched Taylor as he patiently explained to Eddie how to hold the hammer. Debbie was doing small errands and gathering leftover wood to place in the stove's box. I spotted finished shelves, wooden pegs, and five square boxes.

"You surfaced just in time. How's the smoking coming along?" he asked lifting his head.

"Splendid, another hour and we'll finish this batch. You won't have a lot to do tomorrow."

"Great, let's haul some of this stuff inside, and I'll set them up."

Each of us loaded our arms and tagged along behind Taylor up the incline. I shouted to Mai-Li and told her we were in the shed, and she quickly joined us. Soon the wood pegs were up, then shelves for our bedrolls and the bear hide were mounted above the pegs. The last two shelves were nailed on the wall next to the kitchen cupboard. Mai-Li decided it was a perfect place to store our clothes and the kids' books and toys.

"Thanks, one and all," Taylor commented. "I'm almost finished with the wood for the windowpanes, and we can stop for the day. Coming, Eddie?"

I noticed how exhausted Eddie looked, so I quickly intervened. "I was hoping Eddie and Debbie would help me smoke the deer."

It didn't take Taylor long to understand the kids needed a distraction. "Excellent idea, and Carlie, you come with me, and we can finish the windowpanes together."

"Mai-Li is it okay if the kids stay with you while I stand and watch Taylor hammer a few nails?"

Mai-Li smiled and put her arms around the kids' shoulders. "I would love to have them join me; I haven't seen them all day."

"How long have you been doing carpentry?" I questioned Taylor when we arrived at the workshop.

"Since I was a kid, my dad taught me what he knew, and I picked it up quickly. I'm thankful I know the basics, as it comes in handy at times."

Soon the panes were done to Taylor's satisfaction. I ambled over to pick them up when he pulled me into his arms, kissing me gently. This time I didn't complain or push him away, and he stepped back in surprise. I punched him lightly on his arm, and he grinned.

Taylor nailed the blocks over the open window spaces. "We should notice a difference in the temperature right away," he assured. "I'm finished for the day, let's join Mai-Li and the kids in the front yard."

It was comfortable sitting by the fire, the kids chatted animatedly, and Mai-Li smiled and nodded after each comment. Taylor sat next to me and winked when I looked at him. I quickly turned away, though not swift enough to notice the smile on Mai-Li's face.

We finished smoking the first batch of deer meat, then stored it in the burlap sack we had used to carry apples we found while travelling through Vancouver. Taylor hung it from one of the pegs in the woodshed.

We returned to the smoker and placed the uncooked meat in a metal pot, and Taylor placed it in the shed as well. We poured water over the fire, then moved the tepee into the shed, away from prying animals. He commented on my creation, and I told him he wasn't the only one who was a bookworm. I didn't mention my debacle with the Girl Guides, there's only so much ammunition you can bestow on a person.

We hung our coats on the new pegs. Eddie and Debbie tossed theirs on top of the woodpile and rushed inside the cabin. I reached over to get them when Taylor placed his hand on my arm. "Eddie, Debbie," he called. "Come hang your coats up please."

The kids scurried into the shed and sheepishly hung their jackets on the lower hooks. Then they raced back to Mai-Li who was preparing supper at the stove. When she dished out the plates, I noticed she placed more food on Eddie's and Debbie's plates.

The gesture comforted me, yet it terrified me as well. With only Taylor hunting for venison during the winter, it would not be long before we started rationing our supplies.

Chapter Eleven

The next morning Mai-Li and I woke early, we had packed our provisions the night before. Eddie and Debbie were asleep, and we kept as quiet as possible. We had explained to Debbie that Mai-Li would be gone most of the day and Taylor would be watching her and Eddie. Debbie calmly accepted the change in routine, more times than not she changed her mind and if that happened, Taylor would have a distraught youngster on his hands.

Taylor handed me my rifle and pointed out the basic steps on managing the weapon in the event I needed to use it. I sensed his uneasiness as I knew he was agitated I had not started my lessons yet.

"It's okay, Taylor," I assured him. "We should be okay, Mai-Li has her cane, and remember I have my knife."

He shook his head, ground his teeth, and muttered something not nice about my knife. When he noticed the look on my face, he changed the topic. "Follow the creek towards the river and you'll discover a trail that's fairly level, which will make it easier to hike and carry supplies."

Mai-Li and I nodded. She'd finished weaving her basket the day before, and I carried the extra gunny sack.

We strolled through the shed, Taylor stopped and turned to face me, then leaned over and kissed me. I smiled and caught up with Mai-Li who was exiting the side door.

"He's such a worrywart," I told Mai-Li.

"You know perfectly well he has feelings for you, perhaps one day you'll admit it," she responded, and picked up her pace.

We wandered a short distance, and soon picked a new supply of pine needles, then we collected sap and bark from the spruce, larch, and cedar trees. She was delighted when we found a yew tree, split in half by a lightning strike. She reminded me to advise Taylor about it, as he could use the wood to make arrows, and I remember he mentioned he needed a new bow.

We headed deeper into the forest. Unexpectedly, Mai-Li grabbed my arm in excitement. "Carlie looks at all the peat moss."

Having grown up in Vancouver where peat moss grew in abundance, I wasn't too excited about her discovery. She took one of the sacks and packed it with moss. At first, I kept quiet, then I broke down. "Why are we picking moss, it's not as if it's in short supply?"

"They make fabulous dressings and if I had thought about it, I could have used it on your blisters to ease the pain. And, they can be used as toilet paper and menstrual padding, as moss is hygienic. We need to keep this location in mind, and stock up before it starts snowing and gets buried under piles of snow."

I nodded, always impressed with Mai-Li's knowledge of plants and trees.

We eventually arrived at a path that led us to an open field of shrubs. When Mai-Li found a plant that caught her eye, she picked it and handed it to me, which I deposited in the sack I was carrying. When I pointed to a bush covered with berries, she squealed happily.

"Cranberries, Carlie these are cranberries. We need to fill the basket, I can use them in our pancakes, stews, or we can eat them dried. They grow all winter long, what a fabulous find."

It didn't take much to excite Mai-Li.

A few hours later, my sack and Mai-Li's basket were full. "We need to make sure we remember this spot," Mai-Li said. "These will replace the berries Willie ate."

"Are we ready to go and rescue Taylor?" I grinned as Mai-Li straightened her back and stretched. "We still have a long march back, and we should take over 'baby-sitting' duties, and give Taylor a break."

We back trailed for the first half-hour, enjoying the beauty of the woodland, no evidence of wildfires visible in the immediate vicinity.

I asked Mai-Li how she learned about the plants and the trees, and their uses. She told me when her family spent the summers at Blackfoot, her grandparents discovered her aptitude for healing with herbal medicine. One of the chiefs of the Upper-Similkameen People passed his knowledge on to her. They became close friends, and she could not wait to meet with him again. Unfortunately, she and her family did not return to Blackfoot for several years as they owned a restaurant in West Van and needed the entire family's input to support its success. Her three brothers were older than her, and they spoiled her and guarded her fiercely. As more businesses shut down, her parents decided it was hopeless to prolong the inevitable and made the decision to return to Blackfoot. Once they found a buyer for their business and their family home, they would leave Vancouver. They had set their hearts on their children spending more time with their grandparents and relatives, and to learn more about their Chinese heritage.

Then she mentioned the day of the earthquake. She and a few students from her class were on a field trip to the Bloedel Conservatory. Their bus broke down and they were waiting to be picked up by their parents. That was when the earthquake hit, and the tsunami arrived. I told her I was there too and watched it from the lookout. We both lost so much that disastrous day.

We wandered in silence when I heard a dull thud and spotted a squirrel tossing pinecones to the ground. When he detected us on the path, he chattered noisily, warning us away from his food supply. A whisky jack sat on a branch high above our head, and he squawked to announce his presence.

"Mai-Li," I asked. "You speak about your grandparents with so much reverence, as if they were special."

Mai-Li shifted her basket to a more comfortable position, then lifted her head and smiled contentedly.

"In the Chinese culture, our younger people are taught to respect, obey, and care for their elders which should not be perceived as a duty or an obligation. These moral values were lost over time by our people, especially those who travelled to different countries. The World is a different place, undergoing cataclysmic changes in weather patterns, conflicts, global pandemics, and recessions. We have the power to change it for the better, and my grandparents have reintroduced these older philosophies to the people living in Blackfoot. Not each person will be in agreement, and they have the choice to leave should they wish to do so."

I was fascinated by Mai-Li's response, then she questioned me about my childhood. At first, I was reluctant to respond. She waited patiently, then I told her she was lucky to grow up with siblings as I was an only child, and my parents worked long hours at the University.

"Now I understand why you are so lonely," Mai-Li spoke in a subdued voice. For a few moments, silence hung between us. "When you left us after Rusty died, it was a challenging time. We missed your insight, strength, and common sense. You must learn to control the pain and turmoil you carry inside before you can heal and be happy again."

I was troubled by her comments, when suddenly she spotted the willow Taylor and I found, we raced to it, our conversation brought to an end. Soon the gunny sack was so full I found it difficult to lift. Mai-Li told me she wanted to make another basket, and Taylor had mentioned making snowshoes for all of us. With no short supply of the tree in the area, we would not be idle during the winter months.

We wandered comfortably down the trail and approached a magnificent cedar growing next to the path. We paced around the massive trunk, Mai-Li in the lead. She turned the corner, and I followed her and stopped in my tracks. Her basket and its contents were scattered on the ground, and she was nowhere in sight. How could she have disappeared?

Sensing something was off, I dropped the gunny sack, then slowly raised my rifle, and released the trigger guard. Suddenly a rough voice barked from behind me. "Lower your gun and I won't harm your friend."

I turned and stared into the hostile eyes of a man dressed in a buckskin jacket and moccasins. I stepped back in shock. His left arm was wrapped around Mai-Li's waist and in his left hand he held a knife against her throat.

I stood rigidly, my heart pounding. "What do you want?" I demanded. "We don't have anything of value. Let us go."

The stranger snorted gruffly and pulled Mai-Li closer. "First, I'll take your weapon, set the trigger guard and don't try anything funny."

I did as he ordered; he tightened his hold on Mai-Li, then reached over and grabbed my rifle.

"Been looking for a new firearm, this should do nicely," he snickered. "Now turn around and head back down the trail and keep quiet, any disruption from either of you, I'll shoot you both."

I shuffled slowly down the pathway, then he directed me to stop. "Turn right, follow the path that trails the stream. Stay on it and keep moving until I order you to stop. And pick up your pace."

I couldn't believe what was happening. I trudged for a long time, the path narrowed and at times I climbed over jutting rocks. I knew the only way we were going to escape was by using our wits.

Our abductor coughed and spit phlegm into the bushes.

A rancid odour infused the air, and I slowed down. I sidled around a bend; the path narrowed onto an open space, and I cringed when I spotted a dilapidated shack facing the brook. Its back wall and roof leaned against an embankment and the make-shift access was made from deer hide. In disgust, I noticed mouldy animal pelts stretched on sticks buried in the dirt, while decomposed entrails and blood lay scattered on the ground.

The kidnapper motioned me towards the hovel, he reached over my shoulder and lifted the door flap with my rifle barrel, then gestured me forward. I lowered my head and stepped inside. He lurked behind me in the shadows, followed me, then released Mai-Li and pushed her roughly to the ground. "What do you want with us?" Mai-Li requested in a commanding voice, as she stood and faced him.

"Not sure yet, something will come to mind."

My stomach roiled, and I tried not to breathe in the disgusting odour emanating from the uncured hides and discarded animal bones.

I turned and looked at Mai-Li. She placed her hand over the head of her cane, and I understood what she wanted me to do.

"You can't keep us here," I shouted angrily. I sidled to the far side of the shack, drawing his attention away from Mai-Li.

The trapper grunted, then approached me, and I stepped back. "You got a lot of guts," he mumbled. "You're quite a looker too."

I turned my face away and he grabbed my arm. That's when Mai-Li charged. She opened her cane, and the trapper reacted when he realized her intent. He stepped back just as Mai-Li lunged for his face, missing him by inches. He staggered backwards, bellowed, raised my rifle, and pointed it directly at me.

"Don't try that again," he shouted. "Or this pretty lady gets a bullet. Remove your weapon and toss it in the corner."

Mai-Li cautiously obeyed and placed the cane on the ground in front of her.

"Don't screw with me," the trapper barked. "Kick it over to the far side, it doesn't mean nothing to me if I shoot your sidekick, I already got her rifle."

Mai-Li looked directly at me, then she struck the cane, and I watched as it flew and landed against the back wall. The trapper pushed me forward, and I collapsed against Mai-Li. We landed heavily on the filthy floor.

"What do you want with us," Mai-Li insisted. "Let us go, we'll leave our weapons."

The trapper guffawed. "All I need is this rifle, 'pears to me I already got that. Your cane won't do me no good. I could use two women around here, cleaning, cooking, keeping me happy, if you get my drift."

My stomach twisted in disgust, Mai-Li stood, then grabbed my hand, and pulled me up. "You're making a huge mistake," she warned. "If we don't arrive at our camp tonight, they'll come looking for us."

"They'll never find you, 'pears you gals have been scavenging all day, and it's too dark for them to find your trail." He pointed towards the back of the tent. "Now make yourselves useful, I'm hungry."

We rummaged through the supplies thrown randomly on the ground, and it took all my strength to not hurl. We found a pot of leftover stew, and decided it was safer than whatever was buried in the rancid piles of meat.

We heated the food over the coals in the campfire smouldering in the centre of the hut. The smoke was heavy, and I coughed and rubbed my stinging eyes. Mai-Li found a metal dish, filled it, and handed it to the trapper.

I moved to the back wall and sat on a mouldy bear hide, worried sick about Taylor and the kids. It was too dark for him to search for us, and even if he could, the kids could not come with him or be left alone in the cabin, we were on our own.

I fell into a fitful sleep, waking often and shivering in the cold shack. Mai-Li slept next to me, I doubt if either of us would get any rest, and I prayed we would find our way out of this mess.

The next morning, the trapper kicked my legs to wake me up. I was stiff and sore, and refused to look at him. He ate the rest of the leftover stew, smirking as he watched us.

I followed Mai-Li's eye movement and spotted her cane leaning against the wall. I needed to create a diversion. I rose and sauntered slowly to the front towards the trapper. He placed his empty plate on the ground, reached up and grabbed my arm, pulling me down next to him. He leaned towards me, and I pulled back.

What happened next was a blur. Mai-Li edged over to her cane, grabbed it securely in her hand, raised her arm and crept towards the trapper. He lifted his head too late, and she hit him sharply across his face. He cursed and collapsed.

"Grab your rifle and let's go home," she declared, checking to make sure the trapper was unconscious.

I stared in admiration, then grabbed my rifle and rushed after Mai-Li. "What if he chases us when he wakes up," I inquired.

"Don't worry, he won't waken for a while; we will be long gone by the time he does. We'll make sure we cover our tracks."

We tore down the path and found the gunny sack and basket. Mai-Li rummaged through the bushes and found our flashlight. She must have tossed it there when the trapper grabbed her.

We travelled quickly, staying as far away from the edge of the path as possible. Periodically we stopped and wiped away our footprints. By late afternoon, we arrived at the cabin, the door opened, and Taylor met us at the woodpile. He took the gunny sack and one of Mai-Li's baskets.

"I was starting to worry you were lost or got into trouble," he remarked. "Are you guys okay?"

"We'll speak later," Mai-Li answered, when she spotted the kids standing at the door.

Taylor nodded, and we followed him to the cabin. He climbed the steps and Eddie raced towards me and Debbie flung herself at Mai-Li. They were both chattering at the same time, and Taylor finally got their attention and pointed towards the middle of the room. A crude table, the top made from the confiscated one we salvaged earlier, was sitting next to the stove. The legs were made from left-over wood, and Taylor must have felled a tree, sawed the trunk, and made five separate seats. The kids raced over and grabbed a piece of paper and waved it in their hands. They were so energetic; we couldn't catch a word they spoke.

"Whoa, whoa, whoa," I interrupted. "You first, Debbie."

"Taylor made us a table, and I drew a picture for Mai-Li and Eddie did one for you."

"Why thank you, guys. That's nice. Mai-Li, here's your picture and I'll ask Eddie to give me mine."

After complimenting the kids on their drawings, Taylor nailed them on the wall. I leaned over and whispered. "Nice move, what do we do when we run out of wall space, or worse yet, you run out of nails?"

"It brightens up the place and we have the ceiling, and don't forget the shed and the outhouse."

I shrugged, shook my head in defeat, picked up my bag and placed it on top of the table. I gestured for Mai-Li to take over, though not before I grabbed a handful of peat moss and headed to the outhouse.

That evening we asked Taylor if the kids had behaved, and what their reaction was when we didn't return on time. At first, he shrugged, then he sighed and admitted he was up half the night. First, Debbie had an anxiety attack, and he couldn't calm her. She finally went to sleep in Taylor's bedroll next to Eddie, who tossed and turned all night. Taylor eventually got up and read one of his books.

We told him what happened. He growled angrily, and questioned us sharply, demanding to know if the trapper injured either of us. When I told him how Mai-Li disarmed him, he nodded and thanked her. Then he stood and walked over to me, reached down, and raised my shirt sleeve. I glimpsed the imprints of the kidnapper's fingers on my arm where he grabbed me.

"Why is it you always get hurt?" he asked quietly.

I shrugged, and he bent and kissed me. "As soon as you have time, you start shooting lessons and you might as well start learning the finer points of archery."

"Did you overlook tomorrow is laundry day, if you want to take it over, I can start practicing on my own?"

Taylor smirked, then swaggered towards the shed door. "Nice try, but I believe I said as soon as you have time, we'll start after the laundry is done."

The next morning, I washed the clothes in the stream, my fingers numb from the icy water. The kid's clothes were filthy, I pounded them against a rock. To my surprise, it worked. I hoped the creek wouldn't freeze during the winter; it would make my chore a lot more challenging if it did.

After hauling the wet clothes inside the hut, I returned to the stream and filled the bucket, poured water into the kettle, and placed it on the wood stove. It was such a relief to have running water nearby, it made our lives much easier.

Mai-Li strung ropes across the room to be used as clotheslines. The first time the kids accidentally pulled a line down, I hastily got them dressed and shooed them outside.

Mai-Li spent the day drying plants, then she cooked the cranberries in water, and put them in a covered bowl. The sharp tangy smell of the berries made my mouth water, and I hoped she would make a tasty dessert for supper.

The empty shelves beckoned me, so I unpacked the backpacks, folded the clothes, and made a pile for each of us; and I discovered the purpose of the boxes. Our names were carved on the lid, and they were to be used for storing personal items. If anyone was caught snooping in someone else's box, their punishment was to wash and dry dishes for a week.

Taylor spent the day in the woodshop, Eddie lasted about an hour, then came inside and I made him warm his hands over the stove. The days were noticeably colder, and when I went outside to replenish our wood supply, the arctic wind blew across the treetops, warning us of bitter days ahead.

For the longest time, a notion filled my head, and I decided it was time to put it into action. I gave the kids a sheet of paper and asked them to print the alphabet, numbers one to twenty, and their full names, ages, and birthdays.

With no difficulty, Eddie completed my request. Debbie surprised us as she got halfway through the alphabet before she stopped. Then she lowered her head, and meticulously wrote on the paper.

"Debbie Lynn Ross," Mai-Li read, looking over her shoulder. "Whose name is this?"

Debbie looked up and grinned. "Me, silly."

"When we first met, I asked you what your name was, and you told me it was Debbie."

"I know, you didn't ask for ALL my names."

"Oh dear, that was my fault, I asked you wrong."

"That's okay, Mai-Li."

"Are you only eight years old, Debbie?"

Debbie nodded, then reached for her paper. Mai-Li handed it back to her.

"Debbie," I asked. "What day is your birthday?"

She lifted her head, thought a few seconds, then replied, "25".

"Do you know what month?"

"December."

"Wow, Christmas Day, that's wonderful, now we have one more thing to celebrate."

"Uh-huh, can I draw, I don't know my numbers?"

"Of course, go ahead."

I motioned for Mai-Li to join me at the stove, then told her my plan. "I'm worried about the kids not receiving enough schooling and thought we should put aside a few hours each day for reading, math, learning the alphabet, that sort of thing. What do you think?"

"It's a wonderful idea, neither of them has been in a school since the earthquake."

"For that matter, neither have we."

"Then it will be valuable for all of us. You have just been appointed the official teacher."

"That'll teach me to suggest anything new. Then you can be my Aide. I'll let Professor West know, I'm positive he'll be all for it."

And that was how the Rug Rats School came into being.

Chapter Twelve

Taylor was enthusiastic about my suggestion, and every day, aside from the weekends, which was leisure time, he, Mai-Li, and I sat at the table with the kids and taught them the alphabet, their numbers, reading, and printing. Eddie's abilities went far beyond his age, and we soon discovered his aptitude for math. Taylor gleefully took it over, to my relief, as math and science were never my best subjects. Mai-Li gave her undivided attention to Debbie, who practiced the alphabet and numbers and improved daily.

I jokingly told the kids as I was now their teacher, they were to call me Miss Fleming.

"No, thank you," Debbie giggled.

"No, thanks," Eddie answered, after pondering the idea for a few seconds. "I like Carlie better."

So much for that brainstorm.

A few days later, I woke early, it was dark and chilly in the room. I stoked the embers in the stove and threw in a few pieces of wood. I went to the window and looked outside; large snowflakes fell gently to the ground. Listening to Taylor talk about its ultimate arrival had made me nervous as I realized once it arrived we would be snowbound at the cabin until spring thaw. Vancouver did not get a lot of snow, and when it did it usually melted by the end of the day.

I made a pot of chicory and put it on the stove to brew. Taylor stirred and crept from his sleeping bag. He hastily pulled on his jeans, nodded a greeting, and headed to the shed. He had found an old pail with a battered lid buried deep in the pile of debris we tossed outside when we were tidying the cabin which he placed in the shed to be used as an indoor night toilet. Taylor, Mai-Li, and I took turns emptying it in the mornings. None of us relished the idea of traipsing in the darkness through snow up to our waists to visit the outhouse.

The kids woke and when they spied the snow, they grabbed their coats and mitts and raced to the door. We promptly propelled them back to the table and told them to eat their breakfast first, the snow wasn't going anywhere. In the confiscated food Taylor found in Willie's pack was a box of chocolate, and Mai-Li decided to heat half a cup for Eddie and Debbie to share.

Taylor built a long, flat sled from the confiscated wood, and the hill behind the cabin was a perfect place for the kids to slide. After breakfast, and before they disappeared outside, I laid down a few safety rules which I'm confident went in one ear and out the other. They were allowed to play for an hour, then they had to come inside to work on their homework, then they could take another break.

After washing the dishes, Mai-Li and I sped outside to watch. Soon all five of us were taking turns sliding, two at a time, and the kids would scream and laugh when Taylor and I took a turn. The sled stopped a few centimetres short of the edge of the brook, and I buried my face in his back, waiting for the splash.

Days passed and more snow fell. Taylor showed me how to hold and fire my rifle, I told him I would never be a crack shot. He mentioned his main concern was I be able to protect myself should the need arise. He used a bag of blank shells, wisely preserving our live ammunition. He explained blank bullets could still be unsafe, yet in contrast shooting live bullets was hugely different as it would take me a while to adjust to the feel when I fired the gun. I silently prayed I would not have to shoot anyone, or find myself in any type of altercation for something like that to happen.

When Mai-Li and I told Taylor about the yew tree we passed while foraging, he asked me to show him where it was, he had used most of his arrows on our trek and needed to replenish them. Of course, snowshoes were high on his list as well, as he worried about travelling in deep snow while hunting. I took him to the location, and we returned with the two gunny sacks full of bark and branches.

Taylor spent hours in his woodshop, igniting a fire to keep warm. A few days later he lugged in an armload of boards. He set the wood on the floor next to the front wall by the large window, then returned to the shop and returned with more planks. After pounding and swearing and hitting his thumb a few times, we asked him what he was building.

"I've salvaged enough wood from the destroyed furniture to make three beds," he announced. "There's no shortage of willow branches in the area, which we can use to make mattresses. You up to a challenge, Mai-Li?"

"I would be pleased to make them, Taylor," she replied. Then she turned and looked at me. "I'll teach you how to weave."

I frowned; weaving was not high on my list. If I had a choice, I'd rather chop wood or shovel snow.

"Is that my bed?" Eddie asked.

"Half of it is, you and I are going to share. Time for the guys to have some privacy."

Eddie nodded, ran to the shed, and grabbed his sleeping bag.

"Wait, wait," Taylor cried out. "Mai-Li and Carlie need to make the mattresses first, then the beds will be ready. I'll come back with more wood. Mai-Li, I expect you'll be bunking with Debbie, so the smaller bed will be Carlie's."

The next two days Taylor, with Eddie's assistance, installed the beds. He set up Mai-Li and Debbie's bed against the far back wall next to the kitchen cupboards which space we originally used to store our bedrolls, and my bed located on the east wall, was tucked into the corner, close to the front door.

Mai-Li and I worked on the mattresses, it was arduous work but when I saw the finished product, I was quite proud of myself. The kids slept sounder, and everyone was warmer and more comfortable. Taylor used the bearskin rug as his and Eddie's cover, and I gave Rusty's bedroll to Mai-Li for their bed.

Taylor and I returned a second time to the willow tree and with the wood and branches, he and Mai-Li made snowshoes. We spent at least an hour each day practicing; the kids adapted quickly. Mai-Li and Taylor were both proficient as they had snowshoed often when they were younger, Taylor when he lived in Kelowna and Mai-Li when she and her family visited her grandparents in Blackfoot.

At first, I fell so often I looked like Frosty the Snowman. The aggravated look on my face made Taylor shake his head in frustration. "Carlie, it's not that complicated, it's one of the easiest winter sports to learn, anyone having a basic level of athletic skill can do it."

Wrong thing to say!

"Fine," I sputtered angrily. "Then maybe I won't bother to learn how to snowshoe at all, obviously I'm a hopeless case." I turned and headed back to the cabin, only to slip on the downhill slope. I landed heavily, then I felt strong arms lifting me off the ground. I turned and stared at Taylor, who was trying not to laugh.

"I apologize, that wasn't fair. I'll make you a couple of poles which will help you with your balance. I'm surprised you've never snowshoed before."

"I grew up in Vancouver, it doesn't get a lot of snow."

"You're right, I'll be more patient, and we'll work on it together. The reason I'm pushing everyone to learn if for some reason we should have to leave early, then all of us can travel through the heavy snow."

"I'll try harder, but don't expect anything magical. You know how athletic I'm not."

Taylor smiled, leaned over, and kissed me. Mai-Li and the kids heard and saw the entire exchange.

As discussed earlier, Taylor made a fish trap and taught me how to use it. The first time I hooked a fish, I got so excited I dropped it back into the stream. Thankfully, my back was turned; I didn't tell anyone what happened, especially Taylor, as he had enough ammunition to use against me.

Being confined in a small cabin with two rambunctious kids was extremely tiring. We sent them outside as often as we could. It wouldn't be long before the bitter weather arrived, then they would be spending a lot more time indoors.

A few days later, Mai-Li discovered our meat supply was low and decided it was time to replenish it. Taylor suggested I join him, and at first, I hesitated as I had never hunted before. He noticed my hesitation. "You need to learn to hunt, we must keep our meat supply stocked in case the weather turns, and we're stranded inside the cabin for any length of time."

I nodded reluctantly; quite aware I had no choice but to accompany him. We would be leaving first thing the next morning.

We woke early, ate a quick breakfast, speaking quietly to not wake the kids. Taylor checked with Mai-Li to see if she were comfortable being on her own with them in the event we shot a deer or a moose, which would probably be later in the day. We would have to skin and field dress it, and if the terrain were difficult to traverse, we wouldn't get back until the following morning. Mai-Li admitted she would be fine. Taylor suggested she keep the kids nearby, as he noticed cougar tracks in the snow a few days back while he was grouse hunting. Then he handed her his gun, and she took it and put it on top of the cupboard, out of the kid's reach.

We dressed in layers, and Taylor retrieved his bow and arrow and rifle, rolled the two sleeping bags together, then tied them on top of his backpack. I tied the two gunny sacks to my belt, then grabbed my rifle.

"No, leave the gunny sacks here, Carlie," Taylor advised. "I want to take the tarp, I'm counting on shooting a deer or a moose, and we'll need more than the sacks to carry the meat in. I'll fold the tarp tightly, and you can carry it for now."

"Are we going to be able to carry everything back?" I fretted.

"If the load is too heavy, then we'll leave the bedrolls and our supplies someplace safe, return with the meat, then I'll go back for them."

I nodded, then stepped outside on the porch and grabbed my snowshoes. Taylor followed, then we waved to Mai-Li and left.

We weren't gone more than ten seconds when we heard someone calling our names. Mai-Li was standing on the front porch, restraining the kids from chasing after us.

"Nice call Taylor, let's leave before the kids wake up."

"I thought it was a wonderful idea at the time."

"Kids hear, see, and know all. Come on, we have no choice, let's go back and say goodbye, or they'll run after us in their bare feet."

When Eddie realized Taylor was taking me hunting instead of him, he stomped his foot and ran inside the cabin. Debbie, of course, glared, stomped her foot, and took after Eddie, slamming the door. Mai-Li turned and looked at both of us, crossed her arms and pointed at the door.

We laid our equipment on the porch, unstrapped our snowshoes, and entered the cabin. Eddie was sitting at the table, his chin resting on his hands. I went over to him.

"Eddie, I didn't know you had your heart set on hunting with Taylor."

"He promised I could go with him the next time he went."

"Taylor," I asked, turning to look at him.

"Yes and no. Eddie, what I said was you could start hunting with me as soon as you learned how to fire a gun. Right?"

Eddie lifted his face, fighting back tears, and nodded unhappily.

"I'm sorry, right now is not the time for you to come with me. You're far too young to manage a gun. We'll start at the beginning, first I'll teach you how to set traps and track animals. Is it a deal?"

Eddie didn't answer, which was unusual for him.

"Eddie," I pressed. "Is something else bothering you?"

"No, trapping is alright," he answered in a muffled voice. "But I'll be all by myself when you're gone."

"Of course, you won't, Mai-Li and Debbie will be here with you."

"Debbie has Mai-Li, and Taylor will be gone too, I'll be all by myself tonight."

I turned and faced Taylor, then looked at Eddie. "If Taylor and I aren't back tonight, you and Squishy can sleep in my bed. How does that sound?"

Eddie raised his head and nodded solemnly. After Taylor and I hugged the kids three times each, we re-claimed our supplies and weapons and put our snowshoes back on. Hopefully, we would be able to make up the lost time.

After travelling a while, Taylor spun sharply and looked directly at me.

"What?"

"Boy, did Eddie pull a fast one on you?"

I stopped abruptly, my mind racing through my conversation with Eddie. That cheeky devil, he played me again, and I always fell for it. I hope he and Squishy enjoyed sleeping in my bed.

"Wonder who taught him that?" I questioned staring at Taylor's back. I picked up my pace to catch up with him, having to put up with his snickering as we headed into the heavy woods.

I kept up with him as we traipsed down the trails and navigated through the trees and shrubs. A few hours later, he pointed towards a gulch. We took off our snowshoes, strapped them to our backs, then clambered down the sides. When we got to the bottom, it was noticeably milder as we were sheltered from the frigid wind. We replaced our snowshoes, then lumbered through the deep snowdrifts; I lost my balance, and Taylor grabbed me around my waist.

"Sadly, I have no time to dilly-dally," I expressed firmly.

"Touché," he grinned. "Let the games begin."

We trekked for a few hours, then decided to take a break. We wandered over to an enormous boulder and sat down.

"Do you know if any deer are around?" I whispered quietly, not wanting to disturb the stillness.

"The gully ends soon, then we'll be on open ground, which is foraging ground for deer and moose, so remember to keep low and as quiet as possible."

I nodded, then opened the bag, and pulled out two granola bars. "I thought Mai-Li told us they were all gone," Taylor said.

"She had a few left after we confiscated Willie's cache of stolen food. She kept these for emergencies, for times such as this."

We ate the bars, then I folded the paper and put it in my pocket to save for Debbie. We took a long drink of water as dehydration was always a concern. We had a long strenuous hike once we returned to the cabin, hopefully carrying a deer or a moose. Thankfully, there was no shortage of water in the area.

As Taylor mentioned, it wasn't long before we arrived at the meadow. I recognized it as the one we passed shortly before discovering the cabin. We hunkered down and waited. My legs cramped from the cold, and I concentrated on remaining still. Suddenly Taylor pointed to a dark shape standing in the shadows by the edge of the tree line. He leaned his rifle against the backpack, took an arrow from the quiver, and nocked it to the bow string. He signalled he was going to circle to the right, and for me to head in the opposite direction. I crept through the snow, over dead bushes, and reeds, trying to keep as quiet as possible. My stomach was in knots, and my mouth was dry.

I pushed the high grasses aside; a moose was standing a few metres away, ripping bark off a birch tree. I'd not seen many in my lifetime, having lived my entire life in Vancouver, although I was aware, as most Canadians were, how powerful and dangerous these animals were, and should be treated with respect.

My role was to be Taylor's backup, if the quarry did not fall, I was to fire my gun into the air hoping to distract it while Taylor fired a second arrow.

Taylor squeezed his grip, then raised his arms The thud of the arrow as it struck the moose startled me, and I almost fell backwards into a snowbank. The animal lurched, then tumbled heavily to the ground. Taylor left his cover gesturing for me to stay put. He cautiously approached the downed animal. Then he signalled for me to join him.

The arrow was deeply embedded in its chest. "What if she had babies?"

"It's a youngling, probably two years old, and no, he did not have any babies."

"Smartass. So, what do we do now?"

"We'll field dress it and cut the meat, then we'll wrap it in the tarp. I want to dig a deep hole and bury it in the snow for the night, lots of cougars and wolves in the area and it won't take long to smell the blood."

"Aren't we going to try and make it home before it gets dark?"

"No time," Taylor answered, shaking his head. "There are few hours of daylight left. We still have a lot of work to do, and we need to move quickly. We can't stay in the open we have to reach the cover of the trees. Then we'll make camp, and head home tomorrow morning. It's too dangerous carrying fresh meat at night."

We laboured for hours; the youngling was almost the same size as a mature deer. I kept my rifle nearby, as did Taylor. We salvaged as much of the meat and fat as we could, and Taylor rolled the skin tightly, then tied it with a rope. The meat and hide were wrapped in the tarp, then Taylor put on his backpack, and we left the meadow.

Trudging through the deep snow pulling a tarp full of meat was back-breaking work. Taylor stopped a few times to rest, more for my benefit than his. As he predicated; the sun settled behind the mountains, and by the time we arrived at the edge of the forest, it was almost dark. He removed his flashlight from his pack, turned it on and aimed the beam into the trees.

"That's a lodge pole pine," he said, pointing towards a huge tree. "The ground around the base is protected by the branches and is free of snow which will make it easier to dig a hole. The meat will keep during the night."

Then he grabbed his shovel and began to dig. A smile creased his face the entire time and I realized how much he enjoyed himself. Spending his younger years camping, and hunting with his father when he was young, provided precious memories.

Once Taylor decided the hole was deep enough, we grabbed the heavy tarp and pushed it inside the pit. Then I took the shovel from Taylor and began to fill the cavity with the dirt. He watched me for a while, reached for the shovel and handed me his flashlight.

"I'll finish here. We need to start a fire, see if you can find some kindling, a few twigs, limbs, and moss should do, and don't wander too far."

Soon we had a small fire burning, away from the overhanging boughs. Precautions were taken as it was always a probability the branches were dry, even if covered with snow. If it were any season other than winter, we would not have enjoyed the comfort of a campfire burning all night.

I unwrapped two cranberry cakes Mai-Li packed in our supplies and handed one to Taylor. At first, it took me a while to acquire a taste for them, however they were filling.

We sat staring at the fire, our thoughts wandering. Taylor turned and looked at me, and I returned his gaze. Suddenly he reached over and kissed me. At first, I responded, then I hesitated, and pushed him away.

"What are you doing?" I stuttered.

"It's called kissing Carlie, a gesture of intimacy."

"We shouldn't be doing this, you know, acting like..."

"Two people in love."

"I never admitted I loved you," I answered sharply.

The moment I spoke those words, I regretted it. Taylor released me, stood, then turned, and stared into the darkness. "You're right, you've never told me that have you?"

"Taylor please, that's not what I meant. It's just I...."

"WHAT CARLIE?" he shouted, spinning around.

"Stop yelling at me, you know how I feel. I've told you over and over, I don't want to get serious right now."

"That's right, you'd rather live in your angry bubble, blaming yourself for losing Rusty, it's so much easier if you bury your feelings, that way you won't get hurt again."

I hated him for what he inferred, for bringing up such crushing memories. I gritted my teeth and wiped the tears from my face. I rose, then trudged into the woods. He didn't follow me, although a part of me wished he had.

I stopped at a cedar and rested my back against its massive trunk. It was all my fault; I should not have let it go this far. Maybe some of what he expressed was true, I would always blame myself for losing Rusty, it was a guilt I would carry with me for the rest of my life. I needed to talk to Taylor and make him understand how I felt. Living collectively in a small cabin for four months with four other people would be challenging, especially if he and I weren't on speaking terms.

I stood waiting and shivered; I felt the dampness and cold. I realized I didn't have a flashlight, and I wasn't certain which way to go. I drifted in circles, then stopped, cursing my stupidity.

I heard rustling behind me, and a light shone through the trees.

"Lose your way?"

I faced him; my face streaked with tears. "Taylor, I'm sorry, I shouldn't have said what I did, it was hurtful."

"Not any more than what I said to you. I promise I won't do it again, not until you're ready, okay?"

"And if I'm not?"

"You will be when the time comes."

I approached him, and he put his arm around my waist. "Oops, is this, okay?"

I nodded.

"Thanks for being so supportive Taylor, I'm just not at that place yet."

"I don't have a lot of patience, as you well know, when I find someone I want, I go after them."

"I might not be ready for a long time, maybe you'll find someone else you'll care for."

"I doubt it, I'm too ornery, I've chosen the partner I want. Come on, let's call it a night, we have a long exhausting trek facing us tomorrow."

I followed him back to camp. Taylor added more kindling to the campfire.

"Listen to what I'm going to suggest before you punch me," he said. "It's going to be cold tonight; we'll be warmer if we share the sleeping bags, and I promise I'll behave."

I crossed my arms, shrugged, and did not respond.

Taylor spread his bag on the ground as it was sturdier and better waterproofed than mine. Then he tucked my sleeping bag around our bodies to keep out the chill. He spooned me and kissed the back of my neck. "Taylor," I warned. He chuckled and rested his arm on my hip. As I drifted off, I recalled our quarrel. I knew I had feelings for him, only the thought of acting on them terrified me.

Right now, all I needed was time.

Chapter Thirteen

After we arrived at the cabin, everyone pitched in smoking the meat. Assuming we stayed no longer than four months, our food supply should see us through the winter. We discovered an abundance of grouse and rabbits in the vicinity, which would supplement the venison.

Mai-Li taught me how to make moccasins from the deer hide, and after hours of struggling, cursing, and back-breaking labour, on my behalf, we all became owners of a pair. We told the kids they were to be worn inside only, if they wore them outside, the snow and slush would ruin them. Debbie was infatuated with hers, and we finally convinced her to take them off when she went to bed.

The snow fell non-stop, and after school lessons, we tobogganed and built forts and snowmen. Often, I would stop to watch Eddie, invoking memories of Rusty and how much he would have enjoyed being here. Maybe he was with us in spirit, which gave me some comfort.

One day Taylor and Eddie disappeared, and just when I was wondering if I should start searching for them, we heard voices echoing in the distance. We spotted them in the front yard, dragging a pine tree through the snow.

"Is that our Christmas tree?" I asked.

"Yup," Eddie answered happily. "And we can decorate it, after it thaws out tonight, right Taylor?"

Taylor nodded. "Let's haul the tree inside and maybe Mai-Li will make us something hot to drink."

We set the tree in front of the front window, next to the guys' bed, leaving a small amount of room to open the front door without hitting the boughs. We did not have a lot of space to maneuver in the cabin, yet no-one complained. Taylor made a wooden base with a hole in the middle, which held the tree upright, and served as a water reservoir as well.

The kids spent the afternoon making ornaments from the coloured paper, and we taught them how to cut out snowflakes. Taylor was taking a nap, and when Eddie yawned, I suggested he might want to take a nap as well. He jumped off the tree trunk, grabbed Squishy who was resting against Taylor's arm, walked over to my bed, and crawled inside my sleeping bag.

The cabin was peaceful, and I watched Mai-Li as she explained to Debbie how to glue the paper ornaments together with tree sap. I wondered what lay ahead for all of us.

Staying for the winter was a wise decision, it was the reprieve we all needed to heal.

The next morning the kids decorated the tree. I surprised them with an angel I drew and coloured, and Taylor lifted Debbie and let her place it on top. She was so wound-up it took a while to get her settled down.

On Christmas Eve, we sang Christmas carols, and then I told a story about a princess who was lost in the dark snowy woods, and how a prince rescued her. Of course, I threw in a few dragons to keep Eddie happy. I sensed Taylor watching me, and he winked when I got to the part where the princess and prince kissed and lived happily ever after.

"Lucky princess," he muttered.

I grinned at Taylor, then whispered. "Merry Christmas."

"Could be a lot merrier."

"Remember your promise."

"I know, I know," he grumbled as he strolled to his bed.

"Is Taylor, okay?" Eddie asked. "He looks sad."

"He's fine Eddie, just tired, don't forget he chopped wood today, and tomorrow will be just as busy, Santa will be here early in the morning."

Eddie leaned over and whispered in my ear. "You know there's no Santa Claus. He's just make-believe."

"Now why would you say that?"

"After my daddy died, Santa never came back to our apartment. Rusty told me it was cause he couldn't land his sleigh anywhere as all the rooftops were damaged because of the earthquake."

"Oh Eddie, you two boys sure had to grow up quickly, didn't you?"

Eddie laid his head on my chest, and I held him closely. He started to doze, so I carried him to his bed. Taylor put aside his book he was reading, then helped me get Eddie into his pyjamas. We tucked him under the bear skin.

"Sorry for what I said earlier," Taylor said.

"It's okay, I know I'm so desirable you can't help yourself."

"Well, to me, maybe not to others."

"Jeez, now I know where Eddie gets it."

"I taught him all he knows."

"That's what I'm afraid of."

Taylor grinned, then picked up his paperback and marked his page. I looked at it longingly. Since we began our travels, all I read were comics. I told Taylor what Eddie told me about Santa Claus.

Christmas morning arrived, and Mai-Li made a wonderful breakfast of blueberry pancakes and fried moose meat. She gave Debbie an extra pancake, and carved the number "9" on top, and we all sang Happy Birthday to her. Mai-Li gave her a package and she eagerly opened it. It was a T-shirt; I had drawn a doe and a fawn on it and Mai-Li had embroidered it with coloured thread. Debbie was so excited with her gift, she tore around the room, almost knocking over the tree, it took Mae-Li some time to calm her.

The kids drank hot chocolate, the rest of us had our usual cup of chicory. Then Mai-Li handed out cookies to each of us, Debie laughed gleefully and said. "They're all gone, so we better enjoy it, right?"

"No, there's a few more," Mai-Li chuckled.

As we were tidying up, Taylor put on his coat and went outside.

"Where's Taylor going," Eddie asked.

I shrugged, then returned to washing the dishes. Suddenly we heard a knock at the shed door, and everyone froze. "Who's there?" I called.

"Ho, ho, ho. It's Santa Claus. Open the door, I'm cold."

"How do we know you're Santa?"

"I have presents for Eddie, Taylor, Debbie, Mai-Li, and Carlie. Is this the right place?"

"That's us, that's us, let him in Carlie," the kids squealed behind me.

I opened the shed door; Taylor's arms were loaded with gifts. He was wearing his red sweater, and my scarf and toque. He trudged inside and placed the presents under the tree.

"You're not Santa," Debbie muttered. "You're Taylor, and you're wearing your pretty red sweater, and Carlie's scarf and hat."

"I'm one of Santa's elves. He couldn't make it right now, he's busy, I'm making a few deliveries for him."

Debbie nodded in agreement, and Eddie grinned and gave Santa Taylor a high five.

The first present was for all of us from Mai-Li. She made an ivy and holly evergreen decoration, which Taylor hung by a nail over the front door. Taylor had carved wooden animals for the kids, a bear for Eddie and a deer for Debbie. Then he handed a present to Mai-Li, it was a piece of birch wood on which he engraved the words "Peace and Serenity." Mai-Li smiled and lowered her head, as we knew how much those words meant to her. She placed her gift in the centre of the table.

The kids gave Taylor two acorns tied with a red ribbon from Mai-Li's sewing box. This too was hung above the door next to Mai-Li's decoration. It was beginning to look a lot like Christmas.

Taylor was holding two separate presents, everyone in the room was watching me closely. I unfolded the first gift he handed me; it was one of his books, I knew how safely he guarded them, and I hesitated to accept it.

"Taylor, I can't take this," I protested.

"Why, don't you know how to read?" he asked. I made a face, and the kids giggled and pointed at me.

"Can you read it to us later, Carlie?" Eddie asked.

"I don't know, is it okay to read to the kids," I emphasised, turning to look at Taylor.

"It's Peter Pan, I think they can manage it."

The novel was handed around, it had a variation of pictures and Mai-Li pointed them out to the kids, not letting them touch the pages with their greasy fingers.

Taylor then handed me his second gift. I took it from him, and slowly unwrapped it. "It's beautiful, did you make it?"

He nodded, my face flushed red, and I thanked him. It was a necklace made from wood, and the words 'Good to know' were carved on it.

I quickly turned away, then whispered low so only he heard. "You're such a jerk."

I handed it around to the others, and Mai-Li smiled and let Debbie hold it. Then she handed it to Eddie who read the inscription. He turned and looked at me, and grinning impishly, said. "I know what it means."

"Carlie," Eddie said suddenly. "Don't forget our present to Taylor."

I went to my bed, lifted my sleeping bag, and pulled out a package wrapped in one of my T-shirts. I handed it to Taylor, and he sat down and laid it on the table. He gazed at it as if it were a bomb, not that I blamed him, considering the way, I treated him lately. He unwrapped the cloth and stared at the gift; he was quiet for the longest time. "This is stunning," he whispered.

"Carlie made it, Taylor," Mai-Li remarked.

"I didn't know you were an artist; this is incredible."

"Isn't it terrific?" Eddie bragged, as he leaned against Taylor's shoulder. "It even looks the same as you."

"Except for a few snowflakes, and the deer and fawn on Debbie's T-shirt, I've never seen you draw anything," Taylor said, looking directly at me. "What else are you hiding from us?"

"Nothing really, I was supposed to go to art school after I graduated, and as we all know, that never happened. I haven't drawn anything serious since ...you know...the earthquake."

"This is the first drawing you've done since then?"

"Yeah," I answered, as I sat on the edge of my bed. "I sketch pictures for the kids all the time so they can colour them; I don't know who brought it up, we got chatting about doing a portrait of you for Christmas. The only thing I had was the kid's drawing paper, coloured pencils and crayons."

Taylor lowered his head and stared at his gift. "This was when we first met, in the duct at Little Mountain?"

I knew he wasn't expecting an answer. He rose, approached me, bent over, and kissed me. He then hammered a nail in the wall about his bed and hung the picture.

I captured him perfectly. His hands were resting on his thighs; his duffle bag hung from his left shoulder, and his head was raised. I recalled how taken aback I had been with his brooding looks, his long, black hair tied in a ponytail, his dark, smouldering eyes, chiselled chin, and broad shoulders, a half smile on his lips. And that was what I drew, a memory I knew would remain with me for the rest of my life.

Mai-Li instructed the kids to pick up the wrappings and since most of them were our T-shirts, to fold them and put them back on the shelf.

The rest of the day was spent quietly, I read the first chapter of Peter Pan, and the kids were entranced. They begged me to keep reading, I reminded them of the long days ahead and suggested we limit it to a chapter a day. Taylor reminded them he owned other books we could read.

It was a Christmas I would always remember.

Chapter Fourteen

The next few months passed slowly, we dealt with the heavy snowfall, the occasional blizzard, and at times, howling wolves outside our door.

Taylor and I did all the hunting, I soon learned to read animal tracks, and my shooting ability improved daily. He made new arrows from the yew stems and limbs and used them sparingly.

When he tried to teach me archery, I was a hopeless case. I did not have enough strength in my shoulders and arms, even when he gave me exercises to tone my muscles. Mai-Li asked if she could try, and Taylor handed her his bow and arrows. We stared at her in amazement, she never missed the bullseye, then she admitted most of the Chinese, as well as the First Nations people living in Blackfoot, were all trained in archery. She turned to Taylor and told him he was an extremely skilled bowman, as well as a sharpshooter, and he would be held with the highest respect by the Chinese and Similkameen people.

On the milder days, after their lessons, the kids tobogganed, spent time with Taylor in his workshop, or practiced snowshoeing. In late January, the temperature plummeted, and we kept them indoors, reading, playing, dancing, and making up silly plays and acting them out. Our wood supply was low, so Taylor and I devoted a few days cutting down trees and chopping them into firewood. It was bitterly cold, and I wore my two sweaters under my jacket, and was glad I had my toque, scarf, and mittens.

February and March passed, and I understood what it meant to suffer from 'cabin fever.' I would make up excuses to get away from the clamour of the kids and the constraint of five people living in one room. One morning, the sun broke through the clouds, and I told Mai-Li I was going for a short stroll. Taylor waylaid me and handed me his gun, a disgruntled look on his face.

"Don't forget I have my knife," I whispered.

"Carlie, we've discussed this before," he scolded. "Guns are quicker and deadlier. If you come across a wild animal, be it one-legged or two, you might not have enough time to grab your knife. Don't let it happen again."

I took the weapon from him and placed it in my coat pocket. Then I headed towards the creek. I had earlier discovered an enchanting spot upstream, a flat boulder located next to the brook, and I went there often to unwind. I sat quietly, absorbing the rays from the sun. The ice gradually melted, and I heard the rapid drumming sound of a bird as it hammered against a tree trunk. I looked up and spotted a northern flicker, a medium-sized bird of the woodpecker family. I smiled and exhaled, enjoying the sound of the water flowing beneath the ice.

I closed my eyes, enjoying the welcome warmth of the sun. I jerked sharply when I heard rustling in the bushes behind me. Having learned the hard way in the past, I did not intend to stay around to discover what it was. I cautiously slid off the boulder and headed down the path leading to the cabin. A twig snapped; I spun around. Again, I saw nothing, yet I sensed I was being watched. Bears were in hibernation; however, wolves and cougars weren't.

I was reminded of Taylor's advice to always stay calm and not run if I ever found myself in this situation. If it was a cougar, never turn away, always face it, and back up slowly. My heart pounded, and I inhaled, forcing down the icy panic in my chest. I waited; the silence was overwhelming. I continued down the path, keeping my pace steady, at times plodding through un-melted snow. My luck in the past meeting giant cats was unpleasant and it wouldn't surprise me at all if it was a cougar.

I continued at a steady pace, and I knew without a doubt I was being stalked, I slid my hand inside my pocket and retrieved the gun, remembering Taylor's instructions. I released the safety, took a deep breath, turned, and faced my pursuer. Shock vibrated through my body when I recognized who it was. A rifle hung from his left shoulder, and he was holding his right hand behind his back. He approached me, and I watched in horror as he brought his arm around and I realized he was holding a gun. He aimed it directly at me. A cruel smile creased his face, then he squeezed the trigger. I screamed and stepped backwards, slipped, and landed heavily on the ground. I dropped my gun, and it fired, and I wrapped my arms around my head, waiting for the final assault. I heard a voice calling my name, then I was grabbed, and in terror I fought back, kicking, and screaming.

"Carlie, stop fighting me, listen to my voice."

I opened my eyes, then started sobbing; it was Taylor, he leaned over and picked up my gun, then lifted me in his arms and carried me to the cabin. I heard the shed door opening, and Mai-Li speaking quietly.

He laid me on my bed while Mai-Li removed my jacket and gloves. Eddie and Debbie were standing next to the stove, Eddie wiped tears from his face and Debbie clung to his arm. Mai-Li sat on my bed, and Taylor stood close by watching me. "Carlie, tell us what happened?."

I swallowed and looked up. Would he believe me?

"I can't, the kids..."

"Quit pampering them, they're tougher than you think."

I lowered my head, not sure where to begin. "Taylor, it was Willie, at first, I didn't recognize him, he's lost a lot of weight. His hair is long, and he's grown a beard. He was carrying a rifle."

Mai-Li inhaled and shook her head, and Taylor's face turned hard.

"He was furious; he said terrible things. He held a handgun in his right hand. He pointed it at me and squeezed the trigger. It all happened so fast, I screamed, stepped backwards, and slipped on the ice. I remember dropping my gun and it went off when it hit the ground."

I stood and paced across the floor. Taylor approached me, and I shook my head for him to stay back; I knew if I stopped talking, I would not be able to finish.

I walked over to the table and sat down. I wrapped my arms around my waist and rocked back and forth. I started crying again, and I heard Eddie sobbing.

I shook my head furiously. "At the moment he pulled the trigger, I thought I was going to die, then I realized Willie's gun was empty, it wasn't loaded. He was goading me. Why would he do something that contemptible, why?"

I found it difficult to face Taylor and Mai-Li, so I stared at the floor. "Then he grinned and swaggered towards me. I shuffled backwards in the snow; but he kept coming."

I stopped, lifted my head, and turned towards Taylor. "He grabbed my chin, he. . .he. . ." I wrung my hands and gulped. "Then he said, you'll never belong to Taylor; I'll kill you first before that happens."

"Oh, Carlie," Mai-Li whispered. "I'm so saddened you had to go through that."

Taylor's body hardened. "He's dead." Then he ran towards the shed, and I knew he was going after his coat and weapons.

I jumped up and raced after him. "Taylor, no," I yelled, grabbing his arm. "Don't, it's exactly what he expects you to do. What if he's not alone?"

Taylor hesitated. "I doubt if he has anyone with him, but something happened when he traveled back to the Wastelands."

"How do you know that's where he went?"

"When we asked him to leave, the next morning I followed his tracks, he was headed due west, and not wasting any time. You mentioned he carried a rifle; you might recall he tried to take one of the rifles we had, and I told him it was not his. He must have gone back to the train car. What else did he threaten; you started to share something, but you stopped."

"I didn't want the kids to hear, that's all, this is stuff they don't need to know."

"They won't hear if we speak quietly."

"It's nothing," I whispered, trying to make light of the matter.

"If it was nothing, then why are you still shaking? If it's about you and me, then you need to tell me."

My face reddened, and I pointed to the shed. Taylor followed me, then shut the door. I leaned against the woodpile, and he stood next to me. I raised my head and stammered. "He ... he asked if we'd done anything, if I let you touch me, you know."

"And why is that any of his damn business?"

My face reddened. "He said if I did he would come back and show me what a real man can do."

Taylor inhaled heavily, and I sensed his rage. "He's not coming near you; I'll be waiting for him. This time he has stepped over the boundaries, and I will not and cannot condone what he did."

Then he kissed me, I did not pull away. I laid my head on his chest. "This will not happen again," he growled through clenched teeth. "Promise me one thing."

I stepped back, Taylor's promises were never straightforward.

"If I'm not around, and he approaches you, shoot the bastard. I'm sick of his games."

The look of horror on my face was enough for Taylor to pull me back into his arms. "That was an idiotic thing to say, I'm sorry, I'm just so angry right now."

"I know, but we can't be constantly looking over our shoulders, Taylor, that's no way to live. We need to hunt and gather firewood."

"We've survived on rations before, and we have plenty of wood to last us for a while. We can't risk he'll retaliate and grab one of the kids. The five of us need to remain alert and always stay together."

"We can't lock the kids inside, they'll go crazy, it wouldn't be fair."

Taylor nodded. "If Willie went back to the Wastelands, he must have stolen his rifle and probably ammunition from the Desert Rats, then as soon as the trails open, they're going to come after him, and we don't need them landing on our doorstep, not when we are almost at the end of our journey."

I waited for him to continue. "That's why we must leave. It's early March, and the snow will start melting soon. We all have snowshoes, so we can travel through the deep drifts. We need to start packing our bags and supplies."

"Can't we try reasoning with him?" I enquired.

"Before or after we invite him in for a cup of tea and a cookie?"

"Now you're making fun of me."

"A little, just trying to ease the tension in the room."

"Well, it's not working," I replied.

We left the shed and returned to the main room; the kids rushed over, and I hugged them, and explained there was nothing to worry about.

Mai-Li made a light lunch. Taylor waited until the kids were settled at the table, then he strolled to the front window and looked outside. I knew his mind was racing, making plans.

The next few days were problematic, we wouldn't let the kids outside, and during the day, if any if the kids and I went to the outhouse, either Taylor or Mai-Li accompanied us, their weapons ready.

We cured the moose meat, made patties from the plants, and roots we had picked. The dried herbs were ground, and all the provisions were wrapped and stored in the burlap sacks and Mai-Li's baskets.

I often woke in the night drenched in sweat, recalling over and over what happened. I thought I saw Willie's face staring in the front window, hiding in the bushes, and I was terrified he would grab one of the kids.

A few days later, we sat down with Eddie and Debbie and told them about Willie and warned them if he should ever approach either of them, they were never to go to him even if he asked. They were both so quiet my heart ached. I thought they would be happy about continuing our journey, but their reaction surprised me. I needed to find out what was bothering them. Taylor spent hours in his workshop, his rifle always close by. Mai-Li mended the kids' clothes, while I sat at the table with the kids, helping with their lesson, and drawing pictures for them. I put down my pencil, reached across and took their hands. "Eddie, Debbie aren't you two glad we're leaving."

At first, neither of them answered. They looked at each other, then lowered their heads. I waited for them to speak when Eddie blurted. "We don't want to leave here. Can't we stay forever?"

"Oh Eddie, I understand exactly how you feel; I love it here too; however, we need to go where there are more people, and you can go to school, meet new friends, and never go hungry again. Does that make sense?"

"I guess so."

"Something else is bothering you. Can you let us know what it is?"

"Mai-Li will have her grandma and grandpa, but what about Debbie and me. Who will look after us?"

Taylor had just returned to the cabin and overheard our conversation. Mai-Li stopped sewing and they joined us at the table. Mai-Li sat beside Debbie and faced the young girl. "You will live with me forever, and I'll always protect and love you."

"What about Eddie?" Debbie whispered.

I turned and looked at Eddie. "I thought you understood, I'll look after you, and you'll live with me if you're okay with that."

Eddie shook his head stubbornly. "No, I want to live with you and Taylor, not just you."

My face flushed, and I sensed Taylor watching me, his insufferable smile on his face. "I wouldn't have it any other way," he promised Eddie.

"You and Carlie, right?"

"Yes, both of us."

"Taylor," I mumbled. "You shouldn't say that what if it doesn't happen."

"Of course, it will, you just don't realize it yet."

Mai-Li watched intently from the other side of the table.

"You know all of you will have a home with my family," she reminded us again. "The kids will be loved and treated well, and none of us will ever go hungry."

Taylor leaned forward, stared at the table, then he shook his head. "Thank you, Mai-Li it's something to consider, but we can't burden your family, I presume it's not any easier surviving in the Interior than it is on the coast."

"Taylor, Chinese people have been living in Blackfoot for over one hundred and fifty years; I told you their history a while back."

Taylor nodded.

"Those who remained took a different path," Mai-Li disclosed. "They planted gardens and orchards, and eventually, their arduous work paid off. They have established an agreeable rapport with the people of Princeton, providing them with garden-fresh produce, fruit, jewellery, pottery, and more."

I remained silent, my thoughts in turmoil. Mai-Li's offer was tempting yet right now, other matters occupied my mind, and my future living arrangement was not one of them.

Chapter Fifteen

Over the next few weeks, I watched Taylor with interest. He was more patient with the kids and allowed them to try obstacles beyond their comfort zone. Debbie surprised us all, she did not have as many meltdowns as she had in the past, which, I felt, was due significantly to Mai-Li's patience and Debbie's awareness she would never be abandoned.

Eddie had grown over the winter, he was taller, and his red curly hair darkened to dark auburn. He did not cling to me as often as before, and at times I missed his company, I realized he had matured, and it would not be long before he became a young man.

One morning when I stepped into the shed, I found him standing on an overturned stump, staring at his reflection in the mirror that hung over the wash basin. His face was lathered with soap, and when he noticed me, he quickly jumped down and hid his hand behind his back. I approached him and asked what he was hiding. At first, he kept silent, then he brought his hand around; he was holding Taylor's razor.

"Eddie, did Taylor lend that to you?"

Eddie shook his head, staring at the floor.

Taylor overheard me questioning Eddie. He joined us in the shed, and when he saw the razor, he casually took it from Eddie.

"You finished yet?" he asked.

Eddie raised his head in surprise and nodded.

Realizing what Taylor was doing, I turned and left. I heard him reasoning quietly with Eddie, and when they joined the rest of us, I let it be. That evening, after the kids were in bed, Taylor told me he was aware Eddie watched him when he shaved and understood how normal it was for a boy his age to be curious. He suggested to Eddie they could shave together in the future, until he was old enough to do it on his own. I was so glad for Taylor's tact.

The kids outgrew their boots, and as we did not have a second pair to replace them, Taylor tried to salvage them as best he could. First, he cut the toe cap and part of the midsole of each shoe, and when Eddie put them on and wiggled his exposed toes, he groaned, "It's not goanna work, Taylor."

"Our toes will freeze," Debbie complained.

"Just a second," Taylor responded. "We'll figure out something else. Never stop trying, there's always a solution to every problem."

Taylor massaged his chin, shook his head, and studied the boots. "Mai-Li, do you have any of the moose hide left?"

Mai-Li nodded and rummaged through her bag of supplies. She handed Taylor a generous portion, and he cut it into four equal parts, then nailed a piece to the cap and midsole on each boot. The kids tried them on, it kept the snow out and their feet dry.

"You'll need to put on two pairs of socks, which should keep your toes from freezing, and with your snowshoes, you should be okay," I said.

The kids dressed and went outside to practice walking in their boots. Mai-Li and I tagged after them while Taylor stayed behind to put away his tools and clean up. Debbie giggled when Eddie fell into a snowbank.

Each day the sun got warmer, the crust on the snow melted, and the ice covering the stream and along the embankment melted. We spent the daylight hours packing our clothes, personal belongings, and food. I watched as Taylor removed his portrait from the wall, wrapped it in one of his t-shirts, and placed it in his backpack. We filled the container and the canteen with water. We realized we could delay no longer; we would leave early the next morning. Taylor checked the surrounding area and found no sign of Willie, which troubled me. I was still fuming inside, and I vowed I would not hesitate to use my gun if he threatened or came near me again.

The main part of our journey would be through mountainous terrain, climbing steep hills, and being on alert for potential landslides and avalanches. We also had to be on alert for bears coming out of hibernation, they would be hungry.

We woke the kids early, they had to be pressed as we wanted to leave at a decent hour. While Mai-Li fed them, Taylor and I double-checked our provisions. When it was time to leave, we stood in the doorway, viewing the cabin one last time. It was our sanctuary, it protected us, kept us safe and comfortable, and created cheerful memories we would cherish for a lifetime. I silently promised myself if it were possible, I would return one day.

We strapped on our snowshoes, and with one final look, began the last leg of our journey.

Our location was southeast of Treasure Mountain and south of Dear Mountain, and in the distance we spotted their peaks cloaked by heavy mist. We meandered southeast through heavy trees; Taylor was familiar with the terrain as it was his hunting grounds throughout the winter. The kids were not used to travelling long distances and our progress was sluggish. As I was not as proficient as Taylor and Mai-Li on snowshoes, I tired quickly. Watching Eddie and Debbie stomp through the snow, laughing and joking, brought a smile to my face.

To keep the kids from getting bored, Taylor pointed to tracks in the snow, and asked if they could name the animal. Eddie never missed, though Debbie declared one of the tracks belonged to a unicorn. They were both in high spirits, which made our journey easier.

We roamed for a while, Taylor stopped abruptly, and raised his finger to his lips, hushing the kids. He pointed to a huge cedar, and Debbie's face lit up in surprise. A doe stood quietly watching us, then she silently turned and disappeared into the trees.

"Wow," Debbie giggled. "I told you unicorns lived in the woods."

Mai-Li hugged the young girl, the rest of us chuckled, then resumed our trek.

It was hours later before we arrived at the junction of the Tulameen River and the Hudson Bay Heritage Trail. The snow and slush, and travelling by snowshoe slowed our progress, Taylor did not complain, he complimented the kids often on keeping up with the rest of us.

It was decided we would journey a few more hours then set up camp. None of us walked long distances since our arrival at the cabin last fall and Taylor decided to slow our pace for the time being. We passed a few creeks along the way, and I was grateful an abundant supply of water was available. We moved steadily northeast, towards

Lodestone Mountain. We turned north and travelled alongside a creek until we arrived at Blakeburn Road. It was in rough shape as it had not been used in a long time. Over the years, huge cedars and firs fell across the roadway, making it challenging to navigate. At one point we passed the skeletal remains of scorched trees, bringing back memories of the firestorm, reminding us of the unpredictability of the weather changes.

Taylor pointed to the blackened seeds covering the ground. "These are from the fallen trees and are in regrowth. New shrubs, birch, firs, spruce, pines, and cedars, will eventually grow, but unfortunately it will take well over a hundred years for them to reappear."

"You might recall I mentioned the Tanglewood Hills, Taylor," Mai-Li reminded him. "It's probably safer to follow Lodestone Creek rather than Blakeburn Creek, which is a shorter route but in rougher shape, and susceptible to washouts, especially this time of year. Should that happen, we would be forced to retrace our steps. Both streams lead us to the Town of Blakeburn. Our arrival time by either route would be almost the same."

Taylor removed his backpack and laid it on the ground. He took his map from his pocket and unfolded it. He studied it for a few minutes, then he turned towards Mai-Li. "Thanks, Mai-Li. On the positive side, you mentioned we could trap rabbits or pheasants in Tanglewood, which would supplement our food supply, and, of course, the surroundings are magnificent. However, on the negative side, you mentioned there are larger animals in the area, which means we must be on constant alert, and the climb to the top is steep."

Mai-Li chuckled, Taylor grinned and shrugged his shoulders "And since I would rather not take the chance of having to backtrack, we will follow Lodestone Creek. We are headed to Tanglewood, not because of the plentiful food supply, and because the scenery is outstanding, but because it is the wisest choice."

I sighed and gestured for Eddie and Debbie to join us on the trail. We formed a lineup and turned north.

We covered a few kilometres, and I pointed to an accessible area bordering the path. "Why don't we make camp here tonight, Taylor. The kids are dragging their feet."

Taylor waved his hand and headed towards the field, which was partially covered in snow. We set up both tents, using the smaller one to store our supplies. He slept in the large tent with the rest of us and kept his handgun close by, constantly on alert, keeping constant vigilance, fearful Willie would catch up with us. Often I heard him leave the tent during the night.

I rolled over and stared into the darkness. He protected me fiercely, and I knew, if I did not overcome my paranoia of intimacy, I would lose him. I often wondered what I would do after we got to Blackfoot. Taylor and I promised Eddie the three of us would stay together, and somehow, we had to work something out.

The next morning, we woke to blue skies and sunshine. The snow was melting, which impeded our pace; trudging through the heavy slush and climbing steep trails took enormous energy. Taylor instructed us to remove our snowshoes; he tied his and Eddies to his pack. I took mine, Mai-Li's, and Debbie's as Mai-Li was heavily burdened carrying her pack and Debbie's as well as most of the food and herbs and medications. Constantly watching Debbie took most of her energy and concentration.

Before leaving the cabin, Taylor and Mai-Li had discussed leaving the snowshoes behind as everyone would be carrying a heavy load. After a lot of deliberation, they decided to bring them along as Taylor was concerned the snow would be deeper in the higher elevations. It was a wise decision.

Later in the morning, Taylor and I put on our snowshoes and left the trail, we snared a rabbit and shot a pheasant, and with our remaining provisions, we ate well.

As we climbed, I was impressed with the panoramic view, the mountains in the distance were covered in heavy shadows and mist, and several times we spotted deer, elk, and at one point, Taylor spotted a bear cub that quickly took shelter in a tree. The kids were excited, I on the other hand, was terrified the sow would protect her baby if we got to too close.

In the late afternoon, we arrived at a steep embankment. Below us were the remnants of a town, a creek flowed in the background, and snow sifted around the foundations of the abandoned buildings, destroyed over time by nature and the harsh winds. Taylor signalled for us to remain hidden; he rescued his rifle from his pack, then removed his snowshoes and tied them around his waist. He sidled down the bank and trudged towards the outskirts of the town.

I spread the bearskin on the ground, then we sat and waited. I carried my rifle, and my knife was always nearby. Mai-Li toted Taylor's gun and her cane. The kids were silent, knowing what was expected of them. It was well over an hour before Taylor returned. He sat down on the rug and took a cup of water from Mai-Li.

"It's deserted."

"Just our luck, a ghost town?" I muttered.

"Are there ghosts in that town?" Debbie whispered, leaning towards Mai-Li.

Taylor turned and faced the young girl. "That's what towns are called when the people leave. This place is not totally abandoned. I did meet a man who lives by himself. He told me the town is known as

Blakeburn and his name is Pete Johnson, he wears an eye patch and he's also known as One-Eyed Pete. He's an old prospector and trapper and has lived here on and off for over forty years. He's quite a character, and when I told him about our journey, he asked if we would spend the night as he did not often have guests. I said I would discuss it with everyone first, then I'd let him know. I don't wish to impose on him, if we decide to stay, I'm suggesting we set the tents up next to the stream located behind his house."

The kid's watched Taylor, waiting for the verdict, and I realized a diversion was exactly what was needed for them. Mai-Li smiled and nodded in agreement.

As we were strapping on our packs, Eddie pulled my jacket. "Carlie," he whispered. "Does that guy have only one eye?"

Taylor overheard Eddie and replied. "I didn't ask him what happened. If he wants us to know, he'll tell us."

"Is he a pirate?"

"Eddie, stand still," I interrupted. "I'm trying to put Squishy into your pack. And no, he is not a pirate, and under no circumstances are you to ask him about his eye. That would be rude."

"Okay," Taylor instructed, turning to face me. "We're all carrying heavy loads, and the hill is icy, so be extra careful, we don't need any injuries."

I frowned when he singled me out, but I said nothing. I was worried the kids would have difficulty making it down as their packs were heavy, to my surprise it took them a few seconds to join Taylor at the bottom.

"Come on Carlie and Mai-Li," Eddie shouted, waving us down.

We laughed, and Mai-Li grabbed my arm, and we gingerly sidestepped down the hill, giggling when we lost our footing and landed on our butts. The kids thought it was hilarious and cheered as we slid the rest of the way down. Mai-Li and I clung to each other and landed in a heap at the bottom. We stood gingerly, trying to gain our footing when suddenly I slipped on a patch of ice. Taylor was standing behind me and he grabbed me around my waist stopping my fall. I looked up at him, and he returned my stare; I hastily stepped back, aware of an audience.

"All right guys let's make tracks," Taylor ordered, clearing his throat.

It wasn't long before we arrived at Mr. Johnson's cabin. It was constructed of weathered logs, and the cedar shakes on the roof were worn from years of inclement weather. An old corral was set off to the right and I noticed two horses eating hay. When they spotted us, they stopped grazing and drifted toward the gate. One of them whinnied, and Taylor grabbed Eddie's arm before he took off. "Whoa," he interrupted. "You need to ask Mr. Johnson's permission first. Wait until we're inside, and we'll ask him, okay?"

Eddie nodded happily and waved to the horses. I noticed Debbie clung to Mai-Li's hand.

An old man was looking out the window, and he waved when he recognized Taylor. The door opened and he came outside and stood on his porch, then looked at each of us in turn. The kids were grinning from ear to ear, and Pete chuckled. He bowed when he saw Mai-Li and she bowed back. When he spotted me, he nodded, turned, and looked at Taylor.

I was astounded, why did he dismiss me so rudely?

"Is there a place to set up the tent?" I asked, as obviously introductions were over.

He pointed towards the back of the cabin. "Okay kids," I said. "Let's set up camp before we do any visiting, I don't plan on doing it in the dark."

"Can we pet the horses?" Eddie asked.

Debbie swung around and looked at her friend. "No, I don't like horses."

Pete stepped off the porch, nodded, then headed towards the corral.

"Okay Eddie," I replied. "Go meet the horses, but do it quickly, we have work to do."

Eddie followed Pete and Taylor, while Mai-Li, Debbie and I headed towards the creek. We found a flat section of land, most of the ground was bare except for a few patches of snow. We set up the large tent, laid out the bedrolls, and stuffed our backpacks in the corner. Eddie was still absent, however I let it slide, it would do him good to spend time in the company of male companions.

"What should we do about supper?" I questioned Mai-Li. "Do you think Mr. Johnson would care to join us?"

"Let's wait and see," Mai-Li answered. "He'll let us know."

We trudged back to the house; Eddie was alone at the corral patting the horses. He noticed us and joined us on the porch. "I'm sorry Carlie, I forgot about helping with the tents."

"That's okay, I'll let you off this time, it's not often you can get away from us girls. Do you enjoy horses, Eddie?" I questioned.

He nodded his head enthusiastically. "They have names, one is Lucy, and the other is Gus. Can I have a horse one day?"

"Well, it would depend on where we lived, and if we could afford one."

We climbed the steps and Mai-Li knocked on the door. Mr. Johnson opened it, gesturing us to enter. Taylor was standing next to a picture window on the far side of the room, studying an oil painting of a log cabin, the backdrop a mountain surrounded by heavy forest.

I almost bumped into the kids, who stopped in the hallway and stared in amazement. The kitchen was off to the right, there was a round table, six chairs, a wood-burning stove, with a row of cabinets above the sink.

With massive stones surrounding a burning fireplace, and enormous exposed logs along the ceiling, the rest of the room radiated a natural, cozy ambiance. Full bookshelves, and a sizeable bureau, both handcrafted in chestnut oak, a weathered leather couch and chair, with throw pillows and hand-made quilts, and a round scuffed coffee table, completed the furnishings.

I noticed two closed doors at the back of the room, and assumed one opened to a bedroom, and the other a bathroom.

"Wow," Eddie exclaimed.

"Wow," Debbie piped in.

"I take that as the highest compliment," our host acknowledged. "Come in, come in, you're letting all the heat escape."

I quickly shut the door, then we removed our boots and coats, and hung them on the pegs located next to the door.

The kids raced over to the fireplace and sat on the floor, Pete followed them, took a few logs out of the wood box, and threw them on the flames.

Suddenly the back door opened, and a huge Golden Retriever tore across the floor and raced towards Pete and the kids. Eddie's face beamed, and Debbie cowered behind his back.

"Beau, sit," Pete ordered sternly.

The dog stopped abruptly, his legs sliding on the wooden floor. He sat down in front of Eddie and licked his face. Eddie sniggered and threw his arms around the dog's neck. It was an instant attraction between the boy and the canine. Debbie peeked around Eddie's back and Beau gently licked her face.

"Debbie," Eddie broadcast. "He wants to be your friend." Then he turned and looked over to me, and before he could ask, I answered. "No, we can't get a dog right now. We need to find a place to stay first."

Eddie nodded happily. Now that I'd virtually promised him a horse and a dog, I hope we eventually lived on a farm or at least an acreage.

"Mr. Pete," Eddie asked, looking up at Mr. Johnson. "How did Beau open the door?"

Pete bent over and patted the dog's head. "I removed the doorknob, installed a latch in its place, and taught him to lift it with his nose. Then all he does is push the door open and come inside. The latch falls back down and locks the door behind him. That way, I'm not chasing after him all the time."

Pete returned to the table and sat down. He motioned Mai-Li to sit in the chair next to him, then placed me next to Taylor. He poured six mugs of tea, adding milk to two of them.

"Anyone for honey in their tea?" he asked.

Three hands were raised, and I took the sweetened tea over to the kids and kept one for myself.

"Thank you, One-Eye Pete," Eddie said.

I scowled at him, giving him my strictest look. He scrunched down over his mug and slurped his tea. In frustration, I returned to the table and noted grins on everyone's face.

"What?"

"All planned when we were at the corral," Taylor announced.

They all hooted, except I didn't join in. I detested nothing more than being the brunt of a communal joke, and there were far too many lately. Taylor, of course, was usually the instigator and I made a mental note to discuss it with him later.

We passed a few hours discussing the history of the town, how it was founded when gold was discovered and when it disappeared, the residents moved on. Mr. Johnson, who insisted we call him Pete, built his home himself. I questioned about the furniture, and he admitted he was the carpenter. Then he advised he spent half his time trapping and prospecting; his cabin provided him with a home base to stay in the winter months. The rest of his time he lived with his band.

I turned to check on the kids as they were far too quiet; they were both sleeping, and Beau had burrowed between them. I rose and pointed to the couch. Pete nodded and I removed the quilt and tucked it around the kids and their new playmate.

I returned to my chair and sensed Pete was watching me. He gave the impression of being pleasant, the rest of our group enjoyed his company, but for some reason, he intimidated me. He smiled, then turned to Taylor. "I'd like to invite everyone to supper tonight. I have two pheasants hanging in the shed, plucked and ready to go and a root cellar full of vegetables, with a spice cake for dessert. So, what's the verdict?"

"I believe you know the answer to that," Taylor grinned.

Pete gleefully rubbed his hands together.

We sipped our tea quietly, and I savoured the aroma of mint, my thoughts returning to the chicory we drank every night along the trail.

Then Pete turned and looked at Mai-Li. "I am honoured to be reunited with you again. My heart is filled with sorrow on the loss of your family. Your safe return will ease the anguish your relatives and the people in Blackfoot are experiencing."

"Thank you, Pete," Mai-Li replied, bowing her head.

"Mai-Li, Pete," Taylor confessed. "I had no idea you knew each other?"

Pete smiled, not answering. Then he turned and faced Mai-Li.

"I have known Pete most of my life," Mai-Li said. "He is Head Chief and Shaman of the Similkameen Band, who are located on the west side of the Similkameen River; the Chinese reside on the east side. My knowledge of herbs and natural medications I learned from him."

I stared at Pete, then he placed his mug on the table and turned and faced me. He reached across the table and took hold of my hands.

"I suppose you're wondering why I didn't greet you in the same manner as I did Mai-Li."

I looked at Taylor, who was leaning back in his chair, listening closely.

"At first, I wasn't sure of each of your roles. Taylor is the Protector of your group; I feel the reason you have come this far on your journey is due to his strength, bravery and his skills and knowledge in wilderness survival."

I lowered my head, astonished at Pete's insight.

Did I want to hear what was coming next?

"At first, I could not read you, which is why I greeted you the way I did," he continued, when I looked directly at him. "You are talented, and cherish your friends, especially the children. You find it difficult to share your affection with someone who loves you, you must overcome your doubts and fears if you choose to be happy. That choice, of course, is yours."

The room was silent, Taylor leaned over and placed his arm around my shoulders.

"Thank you, Pete, you are exceptionally astute."

"I feel I have upset you, Carlie, and I do apologize. I am too outspoken at times, and living as a hermit, I overlook my manners. Am I forgiven?"

"Of course, there's nothing to forgive, Pete."

"Thank you. Now, let's put those pheasants on the spit, I'm hungry."

I sipped my tea and stared as the tea leaves, settled on the bottom of my cup. Pete's words shook me profoundly, and I couldn't put them from my mind.

I was going to ask him how he knew we were arriving, and he had all the makings to feed so many people, but after his disclosure to me, I decided it was wiser not to ask. I might learn more than I wanted to know.

Chapter Sixteen

The next morning, we left Blakeburn, the kids waved to Pete, Lucy, Gus, and Beau, and did not stop until we reached a bend in the road, and we lost sight of the cabin. The day was pleasant, the sun was high in the sky, and I removed my toque and scarf and stuffed them in my pack. The snow was sticky, and the kids soon adjusted to the snowshoes, and we made excellent time.

The area had several creeks and rivers, and we hiked for five kilometres. We reached a turbulent stream flowing across the road, fuelled by the melting snow in the mountain passes.

"Remove your snowshoes," Taylor instructed. "We're going to cross here."

The kids refused to follow us into the frigid water, and after many failed attempts, it was decided I would go first, carrying my backpack and rifle. The water was frigid, it was only waist high, I raised my rifle above my head, concentrating on not losing my balance or slipping on the slick rocks.

"It's an easy crossing, who's next?" I advised when I reached the other side.

Mai-Li was speaking quietly to Debbie, who was on the verge of panicking. Taylor whispered in her ear, and Debbie nodded, then reluctantly allowed Mai-Li to lift her on his back. She buried her head in his shoulder and clung to his neck. No sooner did Taylor step into the swirling water than Debbie lurched, struggling to get down. Taylor gestured for Mai-Li to join him. She entered the water and soon caught up to him. She grabbed his belt, then placed her hand on Debbie's back to steady her, then waded across in Taylor's wake.

I was uneasy leaving Eddie on his own on the far side, however he was shouting encouragement to Debbie, who turned and waved to her friend. When they reached the bank, Taylor sat on the edge while I pried Debbie from his back. Then he pulled Mai-Li out of the water, and she was at once smothered by the frightened girl. Mai-Li spoke quietly to her, and removed Debbie's boots and socks, which somehow got drenched in the crossing.

"That leaves Eddie, and the rest of our provisions, I'll be right back," he added. Eddie was ready for him and jumped easily onto Taylor's back. When they were halfway across the stream, he shimmied into the water, grabbed Taylor's belt, and waded the rest of the way on his own.

"That leaves one more load," Taylor chattered. "Ladies, see if you can find a safe place to start a fire, we all need to change into dry clothes. We can't take a chance one of us gets sick."

Although Taylor did not ask for my help, I realized the tents, supplies, his backpack, and weapons would make a heavy load, so I tagged along behind him. We strapped the supplies to our backs and headed back.

Shivering in our dripping clothes, we joined Mai-Li on the far embankment. She found a place for our campsite; it was only a short way down the path and away from the wind. "This is an excellent spot," Taylor announced. "We'll spend the night here, change into dry clothes, and hang the wet stuff next to the fire. Set up the two tents, we'll have something to eat, then call it a night. We didn't get much rest last night, not with eating, gabbing, and visiting with Pete."

"I like Pirate Pete," Debbie announced.

We tried many times to get her to call him Mr. Johnson. He told us he admired her brilliant personality and gentleness, and he accepted the name Pirate Pete with pride.

"I do too, Debbie," Mai-Li affirmed. "I knew Pete when I was growing up, I met him on one of my visits to my grandparents."

"Pete is sensitive the same as you," I whispered.

Mai-Li chuckled. "Pete is First Nations and is one of the chiefs of the Upper-Similkameen People. They subsisted here for a long time, history predicts from the beginning of time, mining and trading ochre and chert. Pete is more perceptive than most, and many of his relatives live in or near Blackfoot. He is held in high regard by both his band and by the Chinese."

"And he chooses to reside on his own in an abandoned town?" Taylor asked.

Mai-Li nodded. "He is a man of many talents. As he mentioned, he is a trapper, a prospector, and an incredibly talented carpenter. He is a learned person and knows more about the history of this area and his people than anyone I know. He divides his time between his trapping and mining, and with his band, you will come to know him once we settle in Blackfoot."

Taylor motioned with his head. "I have always enjoyed reading about the history of the British Columbia Interior. You told us some already, before people started settling here, the fur trade and the gold mines provided revenue to the prospectors and fur traders, also a railway was built to bring supplies and people to the area and to transport furs and ore. I imagine some of the train tracks we came across in the Wastelands are siding rails of the original tracks."

Taylor settled in his sleeping bag. "Years back, part of the tracks west of Princeton was destroyed by wildfires and unavailable to the public for a long time. It was known as the Kettle Valley Railway; the rails were discarded, and the gravel beds were restored and made into a trail. Part of the trail goes from Coalmont to Princeton, and I've decided it's the way we'll go. It's flat, with not much climbing, we might come across a few rockslides, however we'll deal with them if we do."

"People, be quiet please," Eddie mumbled. "I'm tired."

"Okay, did I tell you about the long, dark tunnels we have to hike through?"

"Taylor," I warned. "We need him to sleep, not have nightmares."

I rolled over and stared into the darkness. Meeting Pete and sharing his food and stories made an enjoyable day. His prognostication lingered in my mind, was I so effortless to read?

The next morning, while eating, Taylor took out his map. "It's about forty kilometres to Princeton from here, so travelling kid-pace, it will take around three to four days to reach there. As we previously discussed, I believe we should bypass the town as we have no idea how conducive they are to strangers. Blackfoot is close to eleven kilometres southwest of Princeton, and if we have no disruptions, we should make it in one day. Mai-Li will probably choose to go ahead on her own to re-unite with her family, she has harsh news to divulge to her family. We'll make camp and will join her the next morning."

"No, Taylor," Mai-Li declared firmly. "We will go in a group."

"Mai-Li are you definite about this. Your grandparents will have questions, and they might prefer to talk to you privately."

"Taylor, the residents in Blackfoot will know by now what has happened to my parents and brothers. They also know I survived, and I would do everything in my power to return to them."

Taylor nodded, then revisited his map. I let my mind wander. He placed his hand on my knee. "I know you're anxious about Willie, and if he so much as shows his face, he'll have me to contend with."

I placed my mug on the ground. "I know he will try again, and he'll make his move between here and Princeton?"

"I agree, but we are near Mai-Li's family, and knowing how proficient she is with her cane, Willie will be quite aware there will be others in her family who are just as highly trained, in more than just Kung-Fu."

Mai-Li smoothed Debbie's hair away from her face. "Many people in Blackfoot are trained in the Marshall Arts. They are proficient in archery and weaponry, as are many of the Similkameen people. If Willie tries anything, they will stop him."

The look on my face made Mai-Li smile. "My grandparents are influential, and I am the sole survivor of our family's bloodline. Once I am home, I will be closely guarded. When I enlighten them as to what Willie has done, should he try anything again, they will stop him. It would not be safe for him to stalk us."

"Let's pack up and make tracks," Taylor replied in an agitated voice. He must have sensed, as did I, the import of Mai-Li's explanation of her position in her family lineage. There was something else Mai-Li did not reveal, and it would not be long before we found out what it was.

We stayed on Blakeburn Road, surrounded by snow-covered hills. We eventually arrived at an old cemetery. Most of the gravestones were knocked over, and the picket fence surrounding the graveyard was partially destroyed by the elements.

I wandered off the path and into the brush. I spotted a piece of wood buried in the snow and gestured to Taylor. "Look at this old sign I found on the ground, if you look closely, you can make out the letters "Gran" ... something, something, I can't make out the rest."

"Granite Creek Cemetery. There was also a town in the area known as Granite Creek, which was built in the 1800s," Taylor informed. "It was almost destroyed by fire in 1907, rebuilt, and in 1918 it shut down forever."

"Thank you, Professor West."

"You're most welcome Miss Fleming, meet me after class."

"You wish."

I heard laughter behind me, and I turned and looked down. It was Eddie. "How long have you been standing there?"

"I was right behind you guys, and I know what he means."

"Why am I not surprised."

We returned to the path where Mai-Li and Debbie were waiting. "Do you want to detour to Granite Creek and have a look around?" I asked Taylor.

"No, it's probably not much different than Blakeburn, however one day when I have the time, I plan on hiking through this entire area, visiting deserted towns, discovering old trails, areas that were devastated by wildfires, and abandoned gold and silver mines. I'll add Granite Creek to my list."

"Wow," Eddie said. "Are you going to dig for gold?"

"What good is gold in today's world, Eddie? What we need to do is preserve the history of this area, learn how to improve our way of life by living in harmony with nature. I want to author a book about it, and now that I know a talented artist, I'm going to try and convince her to do drawings for me."

Noticing my interest, Taylor's joked. "I'll be looking for a companion, you might want to consider joining me?"

I shook my head in amusement and hitched my pack higher up my back. We silently passed the cemetery, and eventually arrived at the Tulameen River. A bridge crossed to the far side, and from the state of its repair, had not been used in a long time. We walked slowly down the centre, Taylor led, and I took the rear position.

It wasn't long before we arrived at Coalmont Road. We strolled at a comfortable pace, making suitable time. We were surrounded by benchlands, long narrow strips of level or gently inclined land surrounded by snow-covered upper hills. In the distance, we spotted mountains and occasionally passed rapidly flowing creeks developed from the runoff of the melted snow. Suddenly Taylor pointed to a truss bridge in front of us. On the left was a steep bank, and on the right evidence of a rockslide. The wooden rungs were old and weathered and we crept cautiously across. We continued our journey and stopped when we eyed the ingress to a tunnel. I watched Debbie and Eddie's reactions; Debbie was clinging to Mai-Li, and Eddie could barely contain his excitement.

"Okay, here's the tunnel I was talking about," Taylor told the kids. "It is 147 metres long, and it's dark inside. I'll turn on my flashlight, stay together and don't wander off."

Eddie offered to hold the flashlight, which Taylor quickly handed to him. Hauling his bow and arrows, rifle, backpack, and supplies was demanding and trying to find a free hand was not always easy for him. Mai-Li held Debbie's hand, and I slowly approached them. I asked Debbie if I could hold her other hand. I had learned the hard way to never grab her without asking. Sometimes I received a positive response, sometimes not. This time she nodded and took my hand, keeping pace with Taylor and Eddie, swinging her arms happily as we entered the tunnel.

The rays from the flashlight hit the rock walls, creating elongated shadows. Graffiti covered the walls, although I have always hated it, I admitted to myself some of the artwork was excellent.

A few times Taylor summoned Eddie back, he was so fired up he scampered ahead leaving us in the dark. It wasn't long before the curved exit came into sight.

We left the tunnel, and I spotted dogwood trees growing next to the path. I imagined when the snow disappeared, the forest floor would be a canvas of ferns and wildflowers.

"Can we do it again?" Eddie grinned.

"Not today," Taylor answered.

Eddie turned and raced back to Debbie. "My flashlight," Taylor voiced, holding out his hand. Eddie grinned and looked directly at me. "I lost it."

Taylor stared in disbelief; his brow creased. "How could you have lost ...?"

My heart ached, I smiled and blew Eddie a kiss.

"I was just kidding," Eddie giggled as he handed the flashlight to Taylor.

"Smarty pants," Taylor muttered, then stopped, suddenly realizing what happened. He turned and looked at me. "It's just his way of teasing you, reminding us of Rusty."

"I know," I whispered. "He knows I'm okay with it." Taylor reached over and squeezed my arm.

Before us was flat land, and I spotted a few deserted houses and barns. At one time this area must have been farmland, now it was undisturbed and secluded. The trail eventually narrowed, and we found ourselves in a narrow, rocky canyon with cliffs rising on both sides.

"Look," I pointed. "Hoodoos."

"What's a hoodoo, Carlie?" Eddie enquired.

"What is it, Carlie?" Debbie the parrot asked.

"Okay, I took this in school, a long time ago. A hoodoo is a stone column formed by erosion and water. They can be different shapes and colours."

"Cool," Eddie replied, yet it's probable he stopped listening to me after my first sentence.

We wandered a short way down the path when Mai-Li pointed to the red ochre cliffs on our right. "Come with me, there's something I want you guys to see."

We followed her into the brush. She arrived at an abutment and stepped behind it. "Rock paintings," Taylor said. "Do you know anything about them?"

"The drawings were done by the Nicola-Similkameen Indians, and these red marks are war paint. Tulameen means "red earth," the rock dust that was used to make ochre, which they would grind, add to bear oil, and then used as a dye. This is one of the few examples of recorded information on them as their language is now extinct. History reports the last person who adopted this knowledge died in the 1940s."

Taylor was devouring Mai-Li's words.

"As I mentioned earlier when we were visiting Pete, the Upper Similkameen People inhabit Blackfoot as well as the Chinese. They settled on the west side of the river, and a bridge connects the two settlements."

"Let's look for a flat spot someplace around here," I suggested, interrupting them as I noticed the kids yawning. If Eddie yawned when someone was discussing war paint, he had to be tired. "We should set up camp for the night, we can't be more than fourteen kilometres from Blackfoot, which isn't a long hike."

"Sounds good to me," Taylor countered. "You guys sit over there behind the bushes and stay quiet. I'm going to find a sport where we can pitch the tents."

Taylor removed his gear and toting his bow and rifle, disappeared. He was gone around half an hour, then startled us when we realized he was standing behind us.

"Taylor quit sneaking up on us," I remarked cuttingly.

"Then be more attentive, Carlie, you have to be on alert at all times."

Knowing he was anxious about my well-being, I guiltily looked away.

"I found an excellent spot, it's on the left side of the trail and is located by the cliff which will form a buffer and protect us from the wind, unfortunately the grasses and weeds are almost waist-high, so our long-distance view will be limited."

We followed Taylor, and I listened to the sounds permeating from the underbrush. Crickets chirped, and the occasional peep of a bird lightened the mood.

We finally arrived at the site Taylor chose for our camp. Soon we had the tents set up, and a campfire burning. Patches of snow lie in the shadows beneath the cliff, and it wasn't long before the kids were making snowballs. One of them hit the back of my head, and I swung around and spied Eddie hiding in the tall grasses, grinning like the Cheshire Cat.

"You'll pay for that," I shouted, jumping up and giving chase. He laughed, and we ran into the tall grass and weeds. I had to pick up my pace, not only had he grown taller he now outran me. I finally caught up to him and grabbed him around his waist. He wiggled to get free, and I gave him a hug and planted a wet kiss on his cheek.

"Yuck," he sputtered, rubbing his face, "gross."

"Well then don't throw snowballs at me."

Eddie grumbled, broke loose from my hold, and raced back to camp. I straightened and stretched my back when suddenly a hand covered my mouth. I struggled, kicked, and tried to scream; I knew instantly it was Willie; how could I have been so irresponsible; he was probably right behind us lurking in the shadows since we left the cabin.

"Settle down," he ordered.

Angrily I bit down on his hand, he yelped, then backhanded me across my lip. I tasted blood in my mouth.

This time, I had no intention of cowering. I spit on his face, leaving a trickle of blood and saliva.

"I like the new you," he muttered, clenching his jaw. He wiped away the spittle, then he leaned towards me and whispered in my ear. "Spit and fire turn me on."

"You sicko, when Taylor catches you, you won't get off easily."

"Taylor's all talk and no fight, I'm not worried about him."

Before I could get away, he stuffed one of his filthy mitts in my mouth. Then he grabbed my arms and pulled them behind my back, tying them with a piece of rope.

I turned to run, he grabbed me around my waist and pulled me forcefully against his body. "The more you fight, the tougher it's going to be," he warned. "You keep acting up, and I'll grab one of the kids."

I froze.

"Thought that would grab your attention, no more crap, just do as I ask, I'm sick of fighting you."

He pushed me into the long grass, away from our camp. If I dawdled, he grabbed my arms violently and propelled me forward. I knew when Eddie arrived back at camp without me, Taylor would know at once I was in trouble. He would have no problem catching up to us. Yet, Willie did not look behind to see if we were being pursued. Why was he so confident?

I tried reducing my speed; Willie wrapped his arm tightly around my neck. "Stop playing games, Carlie. This is your last chance, try anything else, and I'll hurt you. I don't have anything to lose." Then he shoved me, and I struggled to keep my balance.

It was then I realized how far he would go; he wasn't concerned about me or the kids. His full intention was to seek revenge on Taylor, who from the time he joined our group proved he was stronger and smarter. Because I continuously rejected him, Willie was angry and spiteful, and he planned to use me to strike back at Taylor. He was using me as leverage.

My heart pounded, and my stomach twisted in knots. Willie knew Taylor would not stop looking for me until he found me. I had no intention of making it simple for him, I would not go down without a fight.

Chapter Seventeen

I stumbled through the underbrush, trying not to fall. If I faltered or slackened my pace, Willie struck my lower back with a stick he carried. I clenched my teeth, refusing to show I was in pain. He was obsessed, I could almost taste his hostility, and it terrified me.

Suddenly, he grabbed my arm and steered me to the left. We soon arrived at the trail, and I recognized where we were. We turned right, and I wondered what he had in mind, was he taking me back to the cabin, or had he decided to return to the Wastelands and the Desert Rats; if that were the case, my life would become a living hell.

It might have been fifteen minutes, it might have been an hour, I had no conception of time. We turned a corner and Willie turned and left the footpath and headed towards a pebbly slope. He half-dragged me up the incline, and I struggled to free myself. He growled angrily and pushed me violently. I stumbled and scraped my knees when I fell. My heart raced wildly; and I had difficulty breathing. I choked on the mitten lodged in my mouth.

"Stand up," he ordered. "And don't try that again."

I shook and trembled; every muscle in my body tensed. At last, we reached the top, and I stared in astonishment. We faced a cave. I stubbornly refused to move; Willie shoved me inside, I hit my head against the rounded opening and landed heavily on the ground. We were in a lair, probably home to a bear or cougar. I spotted Willie's backpack on the far wall and his overnight bag spread open in the middle of the floor.

Willy grabbed my arm and pulled me upright; I ignored the agony of my throbbing head. He yanked his mitt from my mouth and untied my hands. My throat was dry, and my throat was raw. I rubbed my wrists trying to regain circulation. Willie shoved me towards his bedroll and forced me to sit. He went to his supplies and returned with his hip flask. He handed it to me, and I took a huge gulp. He grabbed it back and took a long drink. Then he collected his rifle and gun, stuffing the gun inside his belt.

Why...why, are you are doing this?" I stammered.

"Don't pretend you don't know, Carlie. It's pay-back time. The more you struggle, the more fiercely I'll fight back," he whispered angrily. "Now settle down."

"I won't stop fighting you, Willie."

"That's your choice," he muttered. "I'm going to be gone for a while. Don't try to leave, I can see the cave from a long way off, and I won't hesitate to stop you."

"Wouldn't it make this whole fiasco a waste of time if you killed me?" I spat out angrily.

Willie sauntered over to me, he knelt, and I leaned back. He grabbed my chin, squeezing it forcefully. "I didn't threaten to kill you."

My stomach lurched, and he must have noticed how frightened I was. He leered, then turned, and left.

I sat in silence, my thoughts in chaos. It was almost twilight, and I wondered how much time would pass before the sun disappeared behind the cliffs. I would make my move then, a person hidden in the shadows would be hard to detect.

My thoughts returned to the kids. I knew they were safe with Mai-Li and Taylor. Then I thought about Taylor's stubborn persistence, reminding me how much he loved me. Would it take a debacle such as Willie kidnapping me to realize how much he meant to me?

Willie was a troubled person, at times during our journey, he displayed signs of change when he pulled Mai-Li and Debbie from the Fraser River then rowed them to safety, he saved Debbie in the firestorm, and I remembered the time he spent playing with the kids.

Darkness fell, yet Willie did not return. I groped my way over to his backpack, and rummaged through it, hoping to find something to eat. It was empty and I angrily tossed it against the cave wall. He carried a gunny sack when he left, and I realized he must have emptied his backpack and taken all the supplies, as well as his water flask with him. I cursed him bitterly. I shuffled over to the entrance, there was a half-moon, which would provide enough light for me to make my way to the path. Then I heard footsteps outside the cave. I stiffened, if it were an animal, I would not be able to protect myself. An outline blocked the entry; I put my fist in my mouth and muffled a scream. Willie stepped inside, and almost knocked me over.

"Wondered how long it would take you to make a run for it," he mumbled.

"How long have you been standing there?"

"Long enough."

He paced around me and set his rifle and gun next to his bag. He gestured for me to sit, and I reluctantly did as he ordered.

He grabbed his backpack, smirked, aware I had rifled through it and thrown it angrily against the wall when I found it empty. He stuffed the gunny sack inside the pack, and lowered himself to the ground, sitting next to me. I shuffled as far away from him as I could.

I twisted my head angrily and stared at the cave wall. He chuckled at my discomfort, and it was the first time I was afraid since he abducted me. I, more than anyone, knew what he could do.

He dug in his backpack, and removed a piece of dried meat, I reached over to take it, he pulled it back, grinned, and stuffed it in his mouth. He leaned back on his elbows, chewed leisurely, and watched my reaction.

I shivered and felt goosebumps on my arms. He knew I was frightened, and it seemed to arouse him.

"So now you're giving me the silent treatment," he mumbled. "Fine with me, never could stand mouthy broads."

I rested my head on my raised knees and refused to look at him. I remembered the encounter at the cabin when he aimed his unloaded gun at me and fired. For some reason, he enjoyed tormenting me, and I knew one day he might go too far, especially if I constantly refused his advances.

"Get some shuteye," Willie ordered, as he took another piece of meat. "I plan on leaving early."

"Exactly where are we going?"

"There's a nice cozy cabin not far from here, clear running water in the backyard, an outhouse and plenty of chopped wood."

"You don't honestly believe Taylor won't figure out where we're headed?"

"I hope he does; I'll be ready for him."

"Why do you hate us so much? We let you join our group, we treated you fairly, you could have gone to Princeton, started a whole new life?"

"That's partially true, I was treated fairly, but not by you."

"The only time I treated you unfairly was when you deserved it, leaving me on my own without a weapon to protect myself from a wild animal."

"Weren't you lucky Taylor was keeping an eye on you, and saved your hide," Willie expressed heatedly. "From the very beginning you knew how I felt about you, and you treated me like shit."

I stared in stunned silence. This was the first time he had verbally admitted his sentiments towards me. I could never return them, his treatment towards me was harsh and at times cruel, and I could never trust him.

He shrugged and lay back. "I have one blanket; we'll have to share it."

I turned my face in disgust, rose and edged over to the far side of the cave and sat with my back against the wall. If Willie thought he could intimidate me he was wrong.

"Okay with me, it gets cold at night," he muttered. "And don't try escaping, you won't get far."

I hunched my shoulders and lowered my head in defeat. I waited for Willie to fall asleep. Time passed, if I didn't make my move now, I might never have another opportunity. I rose stiffly and inched towards the front of the cave. I scraped my boot against a rock and froze. Willie stirred and muttered, then he snorted and rolled over. I tip-toed quietly towards the opening. The moon was full and provided ample light to highlight the silhouettes of the trees and cliffs.

I turned left and headed towards the rocky slope. If I could make it down to the path, I'd run into the bushes and hide until morning, then head back to our camp.

I took a cautious step, then another. Suddenly I was hit from behind, I landed heavily, scraping my face on the gravel. I opened my mouth to scream when a hand was placed across my mouth.

"You make one sound," Willie warned in a muffled voice, "And it will be your last."

I shook in terror. Willie was lying on me, and I smelled his rank breath; I struggled, scratched, and pushed him; however, he was too strong. He kissed me and I slapped his face.

"You bitch, I should take you right now," he threatened.

I stiffened; having no clue how far he would go, I vowed I would fight him with all my strength. He must have sensed by rage, as he snarled, stood, and pulled me upright. He pushed me towards the cave. I stopped at the entrance, and he shoved me inside and steered me toward his bedroll.

"This is your last warning, don't try it again," he snapped.

I looked at him in disgust, then I scowled and edged towards the far wall and lowered myself to the ground. I was exhausted, and empty inside.

I knew Taylor would be looking for me, regrettably he would not have known we had left the path and was not aware of the hidden cave. He was probably ahead of us on the trail.

I appreciated he was an experienced tracker and once the sun rose the next day, he would soon realize we were not ahead of him.

I was drained, physically and emotionally, yielding to Willie was not an option!

Chapter Eighteen

I woke with a start, Willie was leaning over me, shaking my shoulder. I sat up and pushed his hand away. I had no idea how long I slept; I ached all over.

I stood and worked the stiffness from my back and neck. Willie gave me a drink of water, but no food. I hadn't eaten yesterday and probably wouldn't eat anything until we arrived at our destination. I was aware what Willie was doing, if I didn't have nourishment, I wouldn't have enough strength to escape or fight him if he got mean again.

Willie tied his bedroll on top of his backpack and strapped it on his back. He pushed me towards the exit; I spun angrily, "I have to pee."

"There's a spot over there behind that boulder. Don't be too long or I'll come after you."

I climbed up the gravel slope, then squatted behind the rock. I quickly emptied my bladder and returned to the cave.

We slid down the scree, Willie in front, and when I tripped over loose rock, he grabbed my arm to stop me from falling. I jerked away, his face was harsh, and although I knew I played a dangerous game, I couldn't stand it when he touched me.

We walked for hours; I smelled smoke, and I wondered who might be camping in the area. The reek of burning wood got heavier, and I remembered the horrific firestorm we survived in the Wastelands. "Aren't you concerned about the smoke," I questioned uneasily, turning to face Willie. "The last thing we need is to get caught in a wildfire."

"You worry too much. There's always a fire burning somewhere in these mountains. We'll start to climb soon, then we can see for kilometres and keep an eye on how close the fires are."

I continued to move and tried to figure out Willie's logic. The brushwood surrounding the trees and open fields was so dense it would have made travel almost impossible if we left the path. We hiked until nightfall and stopped periodically for short breaks, then Willie headed into the bush. He pointed to a fallen tree, and I lowered myself to the ground and leaned against the trunk, exhausted and hungry. He handed me his water container, and I managed to take two gulps before he grabbed it back. Then he took out a piece of smoked meat and stuffed it in his mouth.

"Starving me is not going to work?" I said. "I need food Willie, or I won't make it to the cabin."

He shrugged, then grabbed a couple of cookies, and handed me one. I took a huge bite and at once choked. Willie pounded my back, and I pushed him away. I waited a few seconds, then stuffed the rest in my mouth.

"Whose food are we eating?" I demanded.

"Does it matter?"

"It does, and I hope when you stole it, you didn't wipe them out, these are difficult times, and food is hard to come by."

"You think I don't know how brutal it is to survive on my own? If I don't steal from others, I die."

I became angrier by the minute. If he were honest and pulled his weight, and hadn't bullied me, we would never have demanded he leave. The rest of us coped, worked relentlessly, and did not steal from each other. I looked up at him, curling my lips in disgust. "Your scruples are all wrong, Willie, you always looked for the quickest way out, tell me, have you found it yet?"

I wasn't expecting what happened next. He struck me with his fist; I landed face down on the ground. I froze, terrified of provoking him further. My cheek felt as if it was going to explode, I rolled over, trying to focus. Why did I always egg him on, I knew how violent he could be when he was furious.

"Up," Willie ordered harshly. "I plan on camping here; this is as good a place as any."

I struggled to stand, and when he reached over and grabbed my arm, I violently pulled away, refusing his aid. "Don't touch me."

"Suit yourself, you'll change your mind over time. Make yourself useful, set up the bedroll, then gather some kindling."

I almost told him to go to hell, but I bit my tongue and kept quiet. If he so much as laid a hand on me, I swore I would kill him. Lying awake last night, I had suddenly remembered my knife, which was hidden in my boot. I realized Willie had forgotten about it as well.

I pulled his sleeping bag from his pack, all at once I felt dizzy and disoriented; I wrapped my arms around the trunk of a cedar and leaned against it.

"I'll finish," Willie muttered. "You're white as a ghost, go sit down."

This time I didn't argue. I felt nauseous, I raced into the trees; heaved, but my stomach was empty.

I sensed Willie standing behind me, and I swung around angrily. "A man who beats a woman half his size is a coward, Willie, and no matter how often you do it, I'll fight you; I'll never forgive you for what you have done."

"You will in time."

"Not in a million years. I'll never have feelings for you, it's Taylor I love."

The look on his face was chilling, and I realized I'd gone too far. I wiped my mouth with the back of my hand, sat on the ground and leaned my back against the tree. I must have dozed off; suddenly I woke with a jolt. It was so dark I couldn't see my hands in front of my face. I knew it would be foolhardy to try and run, I had no idea where the path was located. My back ached, my face throbbed, and I had a pounding headache. Hot tears streamed down my face; I laid my head on my knees and rocked back and forth. I was hungry and cold, and I was terrified. I curled into a tight ball and closed my eyes.

I slept on and off, shivering in the cold. I had no idea how long I dozed when Willie shook me awake. We were on the path early. I moved slow, not because I was stalling, but because I was weak from hunger and lack of sleep. Every step I took the throbbing pain in my lower back increased. My face was swollen, and I couldn't open my right eye.

Yesterday we passed the red cliffs, the hoodoos, and the open farmland. We must be close to the truss bridge and tunnel. I thought about the dogwood trees surrounding the bridge and wondered if I had a chance of escaping. The huge ferns and shrubs would provide enough cover for me to hide.

My face was flushed, my lips were dry and cracked, and Willie stubbornly refused to offer me water. I knew this was his way of punishing me when I told him I loved Taylor and had no feelings for him.

Late in the afternoon, we arrived at the tunnel and stopped at the entrance. I realized any plans of trying to escape were useless, I had no energy and had difficulty walking let alone trying to make a run for it. Willie motioned me to keep moving, we got to the halfway mark and walked around the bend when he suddenly grabbed my arm. "Quiet, I hear something," he whispered.

I pulled away from his grasp. "You're imagining things."

"I told you to keep quiet," he hissed sharply. He raised his hand to hit me, and I took a step backwards and fell over a rock, landing on my back. I screamed in agony.

What happened next was a blur, I sensed someone in the shadows, then struggling noises, grunts and sounds of fighting close to where I had fallen. I rolled over to the edge of the tunnel to protect myself from flying fists and legs. A horse whinnied, a dog barked sharply, and then a demanding voice ordered them to be quiet. Then I lost consciousness.

I woke to darkness and the sound of a crackling fire. I was in a tent, wrapped in a bedroll. I heard muffled voices, and my heart pounded. I was afraid to call out. Maybe they were strangers and as much as I disliked admitting it, there were worse people out there than Willie.

The flap of the tent opened, and I stiffened, the dark outline of a man blocked the doorway, then I suddenly recognized who it was. He approached me, knelt, and I started crying as strong arms held me.

"It's okay, you're safe," Taylor whispered. I raised my head and kissed him. Light from the campfire outlined his face, he handed me his canteen, and I took a long drink. He physically wrestled it from my hands. "Not too much, you're dehydrated, take tiny sips."

"Taylor," I croaked. "I'm sorry, I should have been more alert, then Willie wouldn't have had the chance to grab me. It's all my fault."

"It's not your fault, stop worrying and get some rest, and we'll discuss this later."

Exhausted and in pain, I closed my eyes. I slowly drifted off, but not before I whispered, "I love you."

The last words I heard were "Good to know."

Chapter Nineteen

I woke and rolled over. Taylor was lying next to me. He leaned over and kissed me.

"How are you feeling?"

"I'm hungry, in pain, and so pissed off at Willie; I want to pay him back for the way he treated me."

"I understand that, first you need to eat, then we'll make plans."

I heard voices and movement coming from outside the tent. "Taylor, is that Willie outside?"

"And Pete Johnson."

"Then that was Beau I heard barking?"

Tylor nodded and stood up. I watched him as he put on his jeans.

"You know, a lady would have looked the other way."

"Too late now, we've slept together."

"You got that right, the sleeping part I mean."

"I'm in no shape to do anything else right now."

Taylor chuckled, then put on his shirt and tucked it inside his jeans.

"How did you find Pete?" I asked.

"He found me; I was tailgating you and Willie when your footprints suddenly disappeared. It was almost dark, and I knew I couldn't turn on my flashlight and give away my position. I decided to keep going, I thought you and Willie were ahead of me and had probably stopped somewhere for the night. I eventually arrived at the tunnel when I heard movement in the shadows, the outline of a dark silhouette appeared in the entrance; my heart almost stopped beating. It was Pete, he was on his way to Blackfoot to drop off his furs and visit his family."

I nodded, then rolled over on my back, wincing in anguish.

"You, okay?"

"It hurts," I answered. "Especially when I stay too long in one position."

"I told Pete what happened, and he offered to give me a hand. He hadn't passed anyone on the trail, and that's when I realized you and Willie were behind me and must have left the path and hidden somewhere along the way. I probably ran right past both of you."

"We did stop, close to where the Indian paintings are. Remember Mai-Li showed us the abutment protruding from the cliff, if you leave the path and walk behind it, there's a gravel slope. Climb to the top, and you'll spot a cave to the right; it's unseen by anyone walking on the trail."

"How did Willie know about the cave?"

"He told me he's been tracking us since we left the cabin, he found the cave purely by accident."

Taylor ran his fingers through his hair. "I should have been more attentive; I didn't give Willie enough credit."

"None of us did. He grabbed me so quickly; I didn't have time to yell a warning. I tried to fight him off then I bit his hand. That's how I got this bruise on my face."

"That son-of-a-bitch," Taylor growled through clenched teeth.

"I kept fighting him, so he stuffed one of his grungy gloves in my mouth and tied my arms behind my back."

Taylor's looked down at me. "Carlie, he is not getting away with this, he's gone too far this time."

"I don't give a damn about Willie, I'm so fed up with his crassness, I wish he'd disappear forever."

"I've never heard you talk like that; you sound angry and defeated."

I nodded in agreement. "That's how I feel right now, but I refuse to cave in to Willie's abuse. It's time I learned to take care of myself."

"I hope you don't plan on doing it on your own."

I turned and looked up at Taylor. "I have someone in mind, if he's willing."

"You keep talking that way, and we'll never finish this conversation."

I smiled and pulled the sleeping bag over my shoulders.

"Pete and I took turns overnight watching and waiting for you and Willie," Taylor continued. "We knew you would eventually arrive at the tunnel, there's only one way out, and that's on the path. We wondered if Willie would decide to cut through the forest, but that would have been suicidal, it's far too dense, and if a person lost their way, they'd never find their way out. We decided even Willie wasn't stupid enough to try that stunt."

"I thought a few times of sneaking away while Willie slept," I added. "But that would have been suicidal, it doesn't take me long to get lost in heavy forested areas."

Taylor smiled. "That's true, now where was I. It wasn't long before we heard voices on the trail. Pete signalled me to enter the tunnel and hide in the shadows. He stayed outside, with Beau, in case Willie tried to get away. I was wired tight as a drum until I heard you scream; that's when I lost it and attacked Willie."

"I tripped over a rock and landed on my back," I whimpered. "I thought Willie was going to punch me again."

"What do you mean again?"

I lowered my head, unable to look at Taylor. "If I slowed down, or mentioned anything that infuriated him, he would hit me. The first time he slapped me, but I kept fighting him, I tried a few times to escape, which just made him angrier. Then, I said something that wasn't nice, and he punched me hard on my cheek. I was so thirsty and exhausted. I purposely lingered hoping you would catch up to us. If I didn't keep up to his pace, he would hit my lower back with a stick he was carrying. It was so painful, I begged him to stop, but he was so angry. He told me he was taking me back to the cabin."

Taylor's clenched his fists, and his face hardened.

"The first night he wanted me to share his sleeping bag, but I refused and slept on the cave floor. I waited until he I heard him snore, then I escaped and was halfway down the slope when he caught me."

Taylor squatted, at first he was silent, then he lifted my chin. "What happened Carlie, did he try anything?"

I bit my lower lip and swallowed. "I struggled to get free, only he was too strong; he kissed me. Taylor, I tried to stop him, I hit him, and he threatened to rape me if I tried to run again."

I cried harder and covered my mouth with my fist. "I vowed if he tried anything, it would be the last thing he did. He had forgotten I had my knife and if the opportunity presented itself, I would have used it."

Taylor squeezed my shoulder and remained quiet.

I heard movements coming from outside the tent, then I recognized Pete's gravelly voice, and someone answered him. I cringed; afraid Pete would bring Willie inside the tent.

Taylor witnessed my reaction.

"Don't worry, I won't let him near you. Roll on your stomach," he instructed. "Let me look at your back."

I did as he asked and winced when he lowered the top of my jeans. He gently touched me, and I moaned, clutching my fists.

Taylor swore angrily, he rose and tore out of the tent. I heard angry voices and scuffling, then Beau's frenzied barking and Pete shouting. I cowered and covered my face.

I heard footsteps coming towards me. The sleeping bag was pulled away from my face and I stared up at Pete. Taylor was standing behind him, he was shuffling his feet, his hands stuffed in his pockets.

"I reckon you're sick and tired of the male species right about now," Pete said. "What Willie did was cowardly and cruel."

I turned and looked away.

"Carlie, I suggested to Taylor I take you to my place, and he can go back to Mai-Li and the kids and continue to Blackfoot," Pete said. "We'll catch up later when you've recovered enough to travel."

I looked at Taylor, and he returned my stare. "Thanks, Pete, I need to go back with Taylor, I've never been separated this long from Mai-Li and the kids, and they must be frantic. I want to be with them when we finish our journey.”

Pete shrugged, and I could tell he was not pleased with my decision. “I appreciate your offer, but please understand, I can’t be anywhere near Willie.”

Pete turned and faced Taylor, who nodded. “I understand your decision, Carlie, I would have made the same one myself.”

“What’s going to happen to Willie?” I asked. “You know if you let him go, he’ll keep hounding us and will try something stupid again.”

Pete rose and stared towards the tent exit. “I’ve been looking for a young man to help me with my traps, I just might put him to work.”

“You’ll have your hands full getting work out of him,” Taylor informed. “He’ll steal you blind and run as soon as he gets the opportunity.”

“Won’t get far, I know these mountains like the back of my hand, and I’ve learned a few tricks in my lifetime. If he causes trouble, I’ll take him to Princeton and speak to the police. Kidnapping and sexually abusing a young woman might earn him some jail time.”

“I don’t want to dump him on you, Pete. I somehow feel he’s our responsibility,” Taylor added.

“From what I can gather, you’ve done all you can to keep him honest,” Pete replied. “I’ll take Willie” he said, making plans as he spoke. "Carlie is in no shape to walk. Taylor, take Lucy with you, she has a gentle gait, and you'll make better time. We'll meet in Blackfoot in a few days."

"What's going to happen to Willie, Mai-Li mentioned he wouldn't be welcome there, and after this stunt, he's more than likely sealed his fate."

"I have a close friend who lives just outside Princeton, he's a lot meaner than me, and won't put up with any guff. I'll take Willie to him and leave him there until we work something out."

"If you believe that's best, I'd just as soon not see him again, and I'm quite sure Carlie feels the same."

"We can't abandon him; he needs guidance and someone to teach him right from wrong."

Taylor shrugged, not answering Pete. Suddenly I was overcome with exhaustion, and I leaned back, resting my head on the sleeping bag. Taylor reached down and felt my forehead. "You have a fever. I'll bring you water and something to eat. Carlie, are you convinced about going with me? We have a long ride ahead of us, and it will be brutal on your back."

"I'll be okay."

Pete shook his head, and I knew he wasn't convinced we had made the right decision. Then he and Taylor left the tent. I heard them talking and at times they raised their voices.

The tent flap lifted, and Taylor returned with a cup of water. "Drink this, I'll be right back with some food."

I was still drinking when Taylor came back holding a plate. "Pete made scrambled eggs and toast this morning. Try and eat as much as you can, you're going to need your strength."

I picked at my food; I had no appetite. Taylor took the spoon and started feeding me. I pulled back, but he ignored me and when most of the eggs were gone, he appeared to be satisfied. He stood and told me he would be back shortly; he was going to borrow some of Pete's gear and saddle Lucy.

The next thing I knew Taylor was shaking me awake. "I'm not convinced you can be moved," he sighed. "I know you don't want to hear this, but why don't you stay with Pete, and I'll go back on my own; I'll make faster time."

The look on my face was enough for him to pull me into his arms. "I'm just anxious about Mai-Li and the kids."

"I am too, and I can't stay with Pete, I can't be near Willie. I won't be any trouble, I promise."

Taylor kissed my forehead, then stood up.

"It's never going to be easy, is it, Carlie?"

I didn't answer, there was nothing to say.

Chapter Twenty

I felt every jolt. Taylor kept Lucy moving at a steady pace. I was sitting in front of him grasping the saddle horn and dozed off. I awoke in alarm when Lucy bolted. I spotted a spooked rabbit as it tore across the path and headed towards the heavy underbrush. Taylor soon quietened the startled horse.

When he noticed I was awake, he steered Lucy to the right and stopped next to an enormous boulder. I sighted the hoodoos in the distance. He jumped to the ground, then lifted me from the saddle. I swayed, then grabbed the horn again.

"Carlie," Taylor inquired, his voice sounded far away to my ears.

"I'm okay, just a bit dizzy."

He placed his hand on my forehead, then swore quietly under his breath. He handed me his canteen, then ordered. "You're burning up, drink this, and here's a piece of dried meat, and Pete's toast from this morning."

I knew better than to complain and took a long drink. I ate a small piece of the toast and gagged when I tried to eat the deer meat. I felt nauseous. Taylor said nothing, and I realized he was angry I had refused to stay with Pete, and he was also worried about my fever and lethargy.

He lifted me into the saddle, and I shivered. He removed his jacket and wrapped it around my shoulders.

"You ready," he asked.

I nodded and soon we were on the trail again. I fought to keep awake, but I was exhausted. I knew we were not far from our camp. The throbbing in my lower back intensified, and I bit my lip to stop to keep from moaning.

"How far away are we?" I inquired. My lips were dried and cracked, and my body felt as if it had been used as a punching bag.

"We're almost there."

I drifted off and had a strange, unsettled dream. I was home in Vancouver and laughed when Poppy dashed across the lawn and startled the birds in the Hawthorne tree. I spotted Rusty in a meadow of wildflowers, he turned and waved, then disappeared. I tried to catch him, but I couldn't move. Willie materialized and I froze. He had his gun pointed at me, I called for Taylor, but I was alone. I drew my knife and pointed it at Willie. He stopped, then stepped nearer, I raised my arm, ready to throw my knife. A mist encircled Willie, the silence was deafening, and then he disappeared as quickly as Rusty.

I stirred and opened my eyes. I was in my sleeping bag in the tent. Mai-Li wiped my face with a cool cloth. She must have put something on my back, as the pain was not as severe.

Eddie was napping with his head resting on my stomach. I reached over and smoothed his hair away from his face.

Mai-Li and Taylor were watching me, I stretched and grimaced, reminded of my pain, and battered face. I looked anxiously around, and I turned to Taylor and asked. "What did you do with Lucy?"

"The sleeping bags were all taken, she'll have to sleep outside tonight," Taylor answered.

Eddie laughed, and I heard Mai-Li chuckle.

"You're such a jerk," I muttered as I looked at Taylor. Then I closed my eyes.

I woke the next morning; the kids were keyed up and boisterous. Debbie, as was her mien, patted my swollen face, then hugged me. I must have flinched as Mai-Li took her hand and gave her paper and crayons and moved her over to the far side of the tent.

I was able to sit for a few minutes and drank half a cup of water and managed to take a bite from one of Mai-Li's pancake.

Eddie finally stirred and refused to leave my side. He tried not to look at my face, and I knew it was bothering him.

"Eddie, I know my face looks bad, but it'll heal."

"Willie did that, didn't he?" he declared crossly. My poor Eddie never spoke in anger;

I was trying to answer him as best as I could when Taylor entered the tent. He must have heard Eddie asking me what happened. He lowered himself to the floor, took Eddie's hand and gestured him to sit.

"Willie is angry and confused, the only way he knows how to display how he feels towards people is by being mean to them."

"I don't want to be his friend anymore, he hit Carlie."

"He did, and I'm sorry he did that."

"Willie needs someone to love him," a voice echoed from the far side of the tent. Debbie was listening and often I was amazed at how much she understood and grasped.

"He does," Mai-Li whispered. "Maybe one day he will understand and find peace."

We sat quietly, each of us lost in our own thoughts.

Taylor got Eddie's attention and asked him if he wanted to help him groom Lucy, and afterwards, he could have a ride. Eddie jumped up eagerly, his mind focused on something different.

I mouthed a silent thank you to Taylor.

"Come on Debbie, let's go see Lucy," Eddie suggested.

"No, 'member I don't like horses."

Eddie shrugged, then took Taylor's hand. I watched the two of them as they strode outside. I spoke quietly with Mai-Li; she knew I was holding back, and one day I would share with her, right now it was too raw.

For most of the day I slept; I woke later in the afternoon, and I watched everyone, deliberating on how much I missed, and loved them. While eating supper, Taylor brought Mai-Li up to date on Pete's offer to take Willie under his wing, and they would probably arrive at our camp late tomorrow morning.

"I don't believe we should wait for them," Mai-Li countered. "Carlie needs immediate medical attention, and personally, I have no desire to meet with Willie right now and I'm confident Carlie doesn't either."

Taylor nodded and turned my way. "You up to more riding tomorrow? It's not too far to Blackfoot, we should arrive late in the afternoon."

Eddie and Debbie were listening intently. "I wanna see Pirate Pete," Debbie muttered.

"You will," Mai-Li promised. "I understand he plans on taking Willie to his friend's place first, then he'll join us in Blackfoot."

The next morning, the provisions were packed, and the tent dismantled. Taylor put most of our gear on Lucy's back, leaving enough room for both him and me. I argued I was capable of walking, both he and Mai-Li insisted I was not ready, and to do as I was told. We did not go far when the pain in my back flared up and I was thankful I wasn't walking.

We kept moving and arrived at a hillside on the outskirts of Princeton. In the distance, we noticed houses, stores, a few churches, as people resembling tiny arts, rushed about. We watched for a while, then Taylor steered Lucy to the right and we headed south. I understood why he was cautious passing the outskirts of Princeton, outsiders were not always tolerated in the Interior. Our vigilance in avoiding contact with people kept us safe so far.

The closer we got to Blackfoot, the more concerned I became. What if Mai-Li's family refused to take newcomers into their community. I understood most of the residents were Chinese and First Nation, and there was always the possibility Taylor, Eddie, and I would not be accepted. I decided there was no sense worrying about the unknown as we still had over eleven kilometres to cover before we reached our destination.

Mai-Li and Debbie walked in front of Lucy, and Eddie walked beside the faithful horse. I knew he was worried about me, and I wished I could comfort him.

We heard moving vehicles and arrived at a two-lane paved thoroughfare. Taylor hid Lucy in the bushes and told me to keep low so I would not be noticed by passing drivers. The rest of the group hid behind a strand of trees. Mai-Li informed us it was the Crowsnest Highway, the road leading to Blackfoot. A secondary route, the Blackfoot

Road, not far inland, came to a dead-end and became a narrow trail. It also took you directly to the town. Taylor told Mai-Li he would be more comfortable taking that route. Unless you were driving in a vehicle, walking along a highway was not prudent, especially if you were a group of young adults and children, riding a horse and carrying supplies and weapons.

"With gas prices being so high, very few people own cars," Mai-Li informed. "There's not a lot of traffic, we can cross the highway almost anywhere without being noticed."

We hurried across the road and headed inland. Most of the snow was melted, and sage and grasses covered the surrounding hills. We eventually reached a river, the water was high and running swiftly. We had arrived at the Similkameen River, and if we followed it south, we would eventually arrive at Blackfoot.

"You mentioned the residents of Blackfoot sold fruit and produce, and other articles in Princeton," Taylor questioned Mai-Li. "If Carlie, Eddie, and I decide to go there, what's the best route to take?"

Mai-Li stopped, then turned towards Taylor. "It's been a while since I last visited my grandparents, they used the Blackfoot Road, travelling by foot or by horseback. Princeton used to be a lot bigger, however climate changes and a struggling economy affected the population. Wildfires became a yearly occurrence, eventually destroying most of the city. The residents contended with massive flooding caused by early snow melts in the mountains. Eventually, the crops failed from the heat and lack of rain, and most of the farms were abandoned. We passed a few of them on the Kettle Valley Trail. I presume Princeton is a different place since my family last visited my grandparents."

"Thanks, Mai-Li. That's a lot to think about. Meanwhile, I'm looking forward to meeting them."

Mai-Li smiled, then looked away, her gaze settled on the river.

"Blackfoot is divided by a bridge separating the Similkameen Band, which is on the west side, and the Chinese who are situated on the east side," she said. "There are hotels, restaurants, stores, as well as houses and schools shared by everyone."

"What, no more icy rivers to forge?" Eddie piped. Mai-Li poked his ribs, making him yelp.

"Mai-Li, how much farther do we have to go?" Taylor asked. She turned and faced him, walking backwards.

"Maybe another hour of travelling," she answered. "Our pace is slow, it's hard for the kids to walk faster, they are getting tired."

Taylor reined Lucy and she stopped. Taylor felt my forehead, I noticed the concerned look he gave Mai-Li. My forehead was warm to the touch, and my back still ached, though it wasn't the intense throbbing as before.

"My family know we are here and have been observing us for a long time."

"Why haven't they shown themselves?" Taylor asked, as he looked around.

"They will when we are closer to Blackfoot. My grandparents are preparing for my return, as will be the rest of my people."

"What do you mean preparing for your return?" he asked quietly, looking directly at Mai-Li. She smiled and gave each of the kids a cookie. We were no longer rationing food.

"Are they going to take Carlie to the hospital?" Debbie asked Mai-Li.

"There is no hospital, Debbie," Mai-Li smiled. "We have healers who will nurse her and make her better."

Eddie was watching me intently, then he reached up and took my hand.

"Hey guy, I'm fine, just tired."

We continued our trek, I struggled to keep awake. Suddenly Mai-Li stopped and pointed. A bridge spanned the river. On the right was a village comprised of teepees and houses and on the left was a larger settlement of houses, buildings, green spaces, and gardens. We had reached our destination.

A line of people was standing along the riverbank. As we passed, they bowed low, and I realized it was Mai-Li they were honouring. A group waited at the bridge.

Debbie clung to Mai-Li's hand, refusing to let go. Instinctively, Eddie stepped closer to Lucy, Taylor lowered his hand and rested it on Eddie's shoulder.

Mai-Li stopped before the group, and a wail emitted from an older woman standing near the back of the crowd. She approached Mai-Li and touched her face, then she put her arms around her and held her. Mai-Li's tears flowed down her face, and I wiped a few from my own. Taylor placed his hand on my leg and squeezed. Then the elderly woman put her hand on Debbie's head, and surprisingly, Debbie smiled and took her hand.

Mai-Li turned and looked at us. "This is Kim Lee, she was our Amah, which means nursemaid. When my brothers and I got too old for a nanny, she came home to Blackfoot to be with our people."

Taylor bowed his head and Eddie looked up at me, and I nodded. He approached Kim Lee and put out his hand. "Hi, I'm Eddie, and that's Taylor, and that's my Carlie."

Kim Lee bowed and shook Eddie's hand. I sensed they instantly connected. Kim Lee bowed to Taylor, then grabbed Lucy's rein, and looked directly at me. She turned sharply and spoke to Mai-Li in Chinese and Mai-Li answered, providing a brief version of what happened. A man, about Taylor's age, came forward, bowed in reverence to Mai-Li and took Lucy's rein. Lucy started trotting, jarring my back, I turned and looked uneasily at Taylor.

"Do not worry." Mai-Li said. "He is taking Carlie to the healers. You may go with him if you wish, Taylor. Eddie, for now do you want to stay with me and Debbie?"

I nodded at Eddie, and he took Debbie's hand. Taylor reached forward and took Lucy's reins from the young man. I clung to the saddle horn, the pain in my back had returned, as had my fever. I leaned back against Taylor, taking pressure off my back. We followed Mai-Li across the bridge and entered the town. We arrived at a pebbled path which led to an extensive park, which I assumed was the town square. The grass was lush, graceful willow trees spread their branches, and apple and cherry trees swayed in the breeze, permeating the air with the fragrance of blossoms.

A regal, elderly couple, stood side by side in the centre of the square. Mai-Li approached them, they reached for her at the same time and crushed her in an embrace. I knew she was finally with her grandparents. They conversed quietly and Mai-Li turned and looked at us.

The older woman nodded, then approached Debbie and Eddie, who were standing shyly behind Mai-Li. Debbie buried her head in Mai-Li's back and Eddie smiled and shook her hand.

Mai-Li's grandmother turned and stepped towards us, then she kneeled on the ground. "We thank you for bringing Mai-Li safely home," she told Taylor. "We are forever in your debt."

Taylor bowed his head.

Then she rose, wandered around Lucy's head, and stared at me. She did not flinch when she saw my face.

"Mai-Li told us you are her friend, and she will never forget your bravery and support in bringing her home to us."

I was speechless and bowed my head.

"First," she continued. "You must restore your health. Have your man take you to our healer. She is expecting you."

We kept up with a woman who appeared before us and gestured at a large building surrounded by trees. When we arrived, Taylor lifted me down, I was suddenly overcome with dizziness and grasped the saddle horn tightly. Taylor lifted me in his arms and carried me inside.

Two women gestured towards a room, and Taylor laid me on a table. Then one of them steered him towards the exit. "You must go, we will take care of your woman."

I looked at Taylor and nodded. Before he left, he turned and looked at me, and I heard him whisper. "Good to know."

Chapter Twenty-one

I stayed in the healing house for three days, sleeping and gathering my strength. My face eventually healed; the purple and yellow bruises looked worse than they were. A salve smelling suspiciously like Mai-Li's was applied to my back, and the pain eventually lessened.

Taylor came for me, and we thanked the diligent women. I asked him what he did while I was healing, and he told me Mai-Li shared our story with her grandparents and the residents of Blackfoot, of how we overcame hunger, ferocious animals, and a firestorm. When she told them about Rusty, they cried, and when she mentioned Willie, the men shook their heads angrily.

We strolled down a scenic street and passed several well-kept houses. Taylor pointed out a few made of logs and added they were the original homesteads the miners inhabited when Blackfoot was first built. The streets were lined with trees, willows, cedars, birch, and early spring flowers bloomed in pots hanging from windowsills. Some of the houses were grander with spectacular gardens.

We passed a sizeable building, and Taylor told me it was the school, and Eddie would be going there with the other children as soon as we enrolled him. We eventually arrived at an impressive structure encompassing the entire block.

"This is Mai-Li's grandparents' home," he informed me. "It's a Sih yuan House, and it circles the entire courtyard. All the doors face south, and they have kept the traditional structure, alternatively these houses have been modernized and many additions were added, such as electricity, heat and running water."

"Taylor, exactly who are Mai-Li's grandparents, and for that matter who is Mai-Li?"

"The best way of explaining is there are four different Chinese social hierarchies, the Shi, Nong, Gong, and Shang. Mai-Li's family are members of the Shi, who are the scholars, officials, highly educated and overseers of the people. The Nong are the farmers, the Gongs are the artisans and craftsmen, and the Shang are the merchants. The beliefs of the Chinese people, specifically those who migrated to foreign countries, changed a lot over the years, and many of their customs and views were lost. However, after the 2021 Global Pandemic and the 2025 Depression, the people in Blackfoot reverted to their ancient ways, and the hierarchies returned. They chose a simpler life; each person is provided for and eventually will have a trade or livelihood that benefits the entire town.”

I knew Taylor was in his element, the histories of diverse peoples and their customs were one of his passions. I took his arm, smiled warmly, and chuckled. “Let me guess, you’ve been chatting with everyone in Blackfoot, and taking copious notes, and one day this information will form part of your historical manuscript.”

“Smarty-pants,” Taylor whispered, as he leaned over and kissed me. “We have to walk faster, or we’ll be late for our visit.”

I looked at him in surprise, then down at my soiled well-travelled attire. “I look terrible, and I need a bath, my hair isn’t combed, I...”

“This isn’t a formal affair, Mai-Li’s grandparents requested we meet with them privately.”

We arrived at a door which Taylor opened. I reluctantly followed him inside, expecting at any moment to be asked to leave. We were in an office, there was a counter at the far end and two men and a woman were sitting at desks. The oldest man, and presumably the one in charge, approached and bowed. No words were exchanged, we were obviously expected. We bowed, then he led us to a door at the back and closed it after we entered.

We wandered down a long hallway, then arrived at another door, then a third, which led us to the main part of the house. Taylor revealed in the central courtyard, there was a shrine set up for ancestral worship.

Mai-Li was waiting for us at the end of the hall. I stared in amazement. She was wearing a dazzling blue silk robe, covered with blossom designs. Her long pigtail was gone, and her hair was piled on her head, with exquisite combs holding it in place. She was the most striking person I'd ever encountered. I moved towards her, and she stepped forward and hugged me, and I relaxed, as I was not sure how I was supposed to greet her.

"Carlie, I am glad you are recovered. Come, my grandparents wish to speak with you."

We entered a generous room, I lowered my head, trying to hide the bruises. Mai-Li's grandmother approached me, and she touched my chin and gently lifted my face. "You helped bring our granddaughter home, and you will always hold a place of honour in Blackfoot."

My face flushed, and I thanked her quietly.

Suddenly we heard shouts coming from a back room. Eddie and Debbie raced across the room, Kim Lee not far behind. She chased the kids and stopped them. They struggled and Mai-Li spoke to Kim Lee, who reluctantly released them. Angrily, she crossed her arms and tapped her foot impatiently.

The kids sprinted to me, and I held them in my arms. I almost didn't recognize them, they were bathed and dressed in clean clothes. Their hair had been cut and washed, and Eddie looked older. Debbie smiled happily and patted my face. I had missed them so much.

"Debbie what a lovely dress you're wearing," I said.

"You're welcum, Carlie."

"Debbie," Eddie said in a no-nonsense voice, "You're supposed to say..."

I raised my finger, and Eddie stopped. He blushed, and I grabbed him and hugged him.

"I missed you so much," I told him.

"I know," he whispered.

"Oh Eddie, don't ever change."

"Okay, are we going home now?"

I looked at Taylor and shrugged my shoulders.

"Taylor," Mai-Li asked. "Didn't you update Carlie about the house?"

"I completely forgot about it. I'll take her there once we are finished here."

We were seated at a long table and served tea and cakes. The atmosphere was relaxed, and I got to know Mai-Li's grandparents. They were cordial and when I mentioned my mother and father and told them what they had done for a living, they were impressed and asked if I would one day continue in the family business. I shook my head and smiled. Mai-Li reached over and took my hand, then explained to them I was an exceptionally talented artist, and their faces lit up. They discussed this topic passionately and I was informed I would be introduced to the artisans, potters, and craftsmen tomorrow morning first thing. They were looking for an artisan, and it appeared Mai-Li's glowing praises were all it took. I glared at her and she smiled demurely.

After the meal, we thanked the hosts and waved farewell to Mai-Li and Debbie. When Debbie realized Eddie was not staying with her, she threw herself on the floor, kicked her feet and screamed. Kim Lee wrung her hands, and Mai-Li and her grandparents bowed, turned, and left the room.

Poor Kim Lee had a long road ahead of her.

Taylor led us to a house a few blocks away from the Sih yuan house. A porch stretched around the residence. There were two bedrooms, a fair-sized kitchen, and a family room, and I smiled when I spotted a flush toilet, bathtub, and shower, which I intended to take advantage of as soon as I was able.

"This is my room," Eddie announced. There was a twin bed, neatly made, a desk and chair, a night lamp, a dresser, and a shelf in the corner holding several books, including the ones Taylor carried with him on our travels. On the bottom shelf was a pile of tattered comics. Eddie added his individualized touch, Rusty's compass was hanging from a hook on the wall, and Squishy was propped against a cushion on the bed.

The other bedroom held a double bed, a night table and lamp, a dresser, and a wardrobe. My drawing of Taylor was hung on the wall above the bed.

I looked at Taylor and he kissed me. "For the time being, I'm living with the single men in their barracks, and unfortunately, they have discovered I know archery, so I am kept busy hunting. Mai-Li told me it would be frowned upon if we lived together, we must marry first."

"Marr...marry," I stuttered, "I'm only eighteen, I'm not ready to marry."

"You'll be nineteen in August; you'll know when the time is right. Hopefully you'll give me your answer soon, I can't wait much longer."

"Shush, Eddie will hear us."

"I know what he means," a voice bellowed from the bedroom.

We both chuckled, then Taylor opened the door, and left.

I stood in the middle of the floor, overjoyed at being together again.

"Eddie," I called. "I'm taking a bath; I might be a while."

He appeared at his bedroom door. "Whew, thank goodness."

Chapter Twenty-two

The next morning, after dropping Eddie off at Mai-Li's grandparent's house, I was introduced to the artisans and craftsmen. I was hesitant at first; their patience and abilities impressed me, and I soon felt at ease drawing and painting again. A few days later, Taylor and I went for a walk, and we crossed the bridge and walked to the village. I met several Similkameen people who were artists and craftsmen. Artistic people were honoured for their skills by both the First Nations people and the Chinese.

I spotted Pete, and three older men, sitting at a campfire. Beau was sprawled next to him, and when the friendly dog spotted me, he raced over, almost knocking me over in his excitement. He licked my hand, and I scratched his ears and face, then he trotted back to the fire.

Pete gestured me over and I anxiously approached him. "Carlie, it is nice to meet with you again. You are recovering?"

"Yes, thank you, Pete. The healers took good care of me."

"Please sit, we need to discuss an important matter. It is about Willie."

I must have flinched, as he reached over and took my hands.

"He is here, it has been decided we will keep him with us until he is older and has learned the right path in becoming a trustworthy man. He will not be allowed to cross the bridge."

I suddenly felt light-headed, and Pete noticed my anxiety. He nodded to someone standing behind me. I turned sharply, there was no one there.

"You promised to take him to your friend in Princeton, why is he here?" I asked, turning to face him.

"Willie and I had a long discussion, he is confused and angry, and sorry for what he did. If given enough time, I feel he will grow and mature."

"He has no morals," I answered heatedly. "He is mean, cruel, and a bully. Pete, I cannot accept this."

"Carlie, we must talk about..."

"No, I will not discuss this with you," I interrupted, "I have to go."

I stood and spun around, barrelling into Taylor. I wrapped my arms around his waist, my face hot with tears.

"Carlie," he spoke gently. "Look at me."

I shook my head and pressed against his body. He spoke to Pete, then we turned and left.

I was upset and disappointed in Pete's betrayal. I thought he understood the way I felt about Willie.

Taylor led me away from the settlement, and we wandered through the forest and the open fields. We discovered a quiet grove, with wildflowers growing along the bank of a stream, and willows and aspens covered in early buds.

We sat on the grass, and Taylor took me in his arms, I clung to him, wiping away my tears. We sat for a long time, then he released me and waited.

I looked directly at him, and I sensed his love, and something more. He was not being entirely honest, there was something he wasn't telling me.

"You knew about this, didn't you, you had it arranged with Pete, that's why you took me to the village."

He stared into the forest, then he turned towards me, and I dreaded his next words.

"Pete told me about his change of plans a few days ago. We discussed it in length, and I listened carefully. He is a wise man and Shaman of the Similkameen People. He is to be treated with respect and honour."

"I appreciate that, but I don't understand why he has forgiven Willie."

"You know the story of Willie's upbringing, and the only way he knew how to survive was to steal from and bully others."

"I'm not referring to that and you know it, that kind of behaviour can be forgiven. He attacked me, threatened me, and abused me. How can I exonerate him or forgive him?"

"You need to talk to him... wait, wait hear me out. You'll never achieve peace if you don't try. I don't want this to come between us, Carlie, we must start with a fresh slate, or we'll never be happy. Do you understand what I am saying?"

I waited silently, my mouth dry and my stomach in knots. Taylor was giving me an ultimatum, I was to meet and talk to Willie and find the strength to pardon him, and if I didn't, I would lose Taylor.

What I did next took all my strength, I stood, looked down at Taylor and said. "I'm sorry, I regret you chose Willie over me. I can never forgive your treachery; I don't want to see you again."

Then I walked away, my body stiff, while tears streamed down my face.

Chapter Twenty-three

I stayed in my bedroom, and I knew Kim Lee was watching Eddie. I ate no food and refused to talk or meet with anyone. I loved Taylor and I also despised him for what he had done.

Days passed and I kept to my bed, wrapped in my blankets; late one afternoon, I heard a heavy knock at the front door.

"Carlie," a muffled voice ordered. "Please open the door."

Lethargically, I pushed back the covers and sat up. I left the bed, grabbed my robe, and walked into the living room.

"Go away," I exclaimed. "I don't want to see anyone right now."

"You will allow me to enter."

I inhaled, realizing it was Mai-Li, and she was not pleading, she was ordering.

I took a deep breath, and slowly opened the door. Mai-Li nodded regally and entered the room. I spotted two guards standing stoically on the porch. I closed the door, but not before I noticed the irritated looks on their faces.

I offered my chair to Mai-Li. She sat down, and I stayed standing, staring nervously at the floor.

"Carlie, I have spoken with both Taylor and Chief Johnson. They are concerned about you. I know you are finding it difficult to accept their suggestions, not only is it for your good, but for the rest of us as well."

I did not raise my head, I closed my eyes and remained silent.

"Do you remember Pete's words when you first met him at his cabin? He said you have difficulty sharing your affection with someone who loves you, and you must overcome your doubts and fears."

"It has nothing to do with this," I answered, raising my head, and looking directly at Mai-Li.

"It does, Carlie, your decisions you make now will affect your future relationship with Taylor. We love you and want you to find happiness, you know what you must do, you must confront Willie and absolve him."

I stubbornly shook my head. "I can't Mai-Li. I don't ever want to speak to him again. I don't trust him, and I loathe what he did to me."

"I, as well, condemn what he did, as do all of us. However, if you don't forgive him, how can he, or any of us, find peace?"

I looked into Mai-Li's eyes. I knew what she wanted me to say, and if I didn't, I would lose her friendship and eventually, Taylor's love.

"I can't, Mai-Li. I refuse to have a discussion with Willie, I will never vindicate his behaviour."

'This is your last word," Mai-Li asked, sighing heavily.

I did not respond. Mai-Li shook her head in resignation, then she rose and walked to the door. She turned and faced me. "Carlie, I regret you feel this way. Unfortunately, I cannot allow you to remain in Blackfoot. We have no room here for resentment and malevolence. I must ask you to leave."

I covered my mouth with my hands, shocked by her ultimatum.

"Does this include Taylor and Eddie as well as me?"

"Carlie, Taylor is not here. He left days ago, with Chief Johnson. I thought you knew?"

I grabbed the back of the chair, fighting to catch my breath. How could Taylor leave without telling me?

"What about Eddie?"

"He's with me and my family. Taylor asked us to take care of him until he returns, he does not know how long he will be gone."

"Mai-Li, I thought we were friends; Taylor is old enough to make his own decisions and his decision to leave and not tell me was his alone. However, Eddie is a young boy, you cannot take him away from me."

Mai-Li straightened her back and opened the door. The last words she spoke, left me empty and broken.

"Heal yourself, Carlie, you are in no condition to care for a young boy on your own. If you and Taylor were meant to be together, you will find each other again. Go in peace my friend, and when the time is right, come back to us."

Then she quietly opened the door and bolted it behind her. I fell to the floor, wrapped my arms around my waist and sobbed. At that moment, I experienced deep anger and shock, my two best friends had betrayed me and violated my trust.

I would do everything in my power to get Eddie back, no matter what it took. And then we would leave Blackfoot, and never return.

Chapter Twenty-four

I tried to see Eddie, requesting an audience with Mai-Li but her guards refused to let me enter the Sih yuan House. I returned every day for a week; my pleas ignored. The emptiness and numbness deepened; I had difficulty sleeping. I had to keep trying, losing Eddie would be as shattering to me as when I lost Rusty.

I approached the Sih yuan House and stood outside the back entrance. I heard my name being called. I turned sharply and spotted Mai-Li standing in the gardens, surrounded by her guards, holding Eddie's hand. She released him and he raced over to me, and we held each other tightly.

"Carlie," Eddie said, looking towards Mai-Li. "I can't see you again, not until you get better."

It was at that point I realized I had lost him, and I had to leave without him, there was no place for me in Blackfoot.

"Eddie, I must go, I know I can't take you with me. You need to be with Debbie, as she relies on you very much. You will be happy here, you will go to school and learn, and you will be loved by Mai-Li and her family."

Eddie nodded and spoke. "I know you are still mad at Willie, and I am too. I'm sorry Taylor did not tell you he was leaving, because I know he wanted you to go with him and help him with his book."

Eddie started crying, and I grabbed him and held him close. The guards were walking towards us, and I knew it was time to say goodbye to my wonderful, special boy. I hugged him and kissed his cheek, wiping away the tears.

"I love you Eddie, I will always love you. Be strong and brave. Don't forget me."

"Promise me you will come back." Then he turned and walked away. At that moment I thought I would never see him again.

I returned to the house and dragged my backpack out of the cupboard. I packed my clothes and personal items and tied my sleeping bag on top. I found one of the water containers and filled it. I would take only what I brought with me. It was then I realized my drawing I had done of Taylor was gone. All of Eddie's belongings had been removed, along with Squishy. The last thing I did was place Taylor's Christmas gifts he had given me, Peter Pan, and the wooden necklace, on the kitchen table. I did not want anything that reminded me of him. I took one last look around, nothing remained in the empty house to indicate I had lived here. I retrieved my rifle, and discovered I had a box of ammunition left. I reached down and touched my knife, which I always kept hidden in my boot.

I shifted my backpack higher, slung my rifle over my shoulder and left. I did not pass anyone in the streets, I arrived at the bridge and kept walking. When I reached the far side, I stopped and looked around one last time. There was no-one in sight, the silence cloaked me, I turned right, heading north, with no destination in mind.

I don't recall how long I walked before I heard my name being called.

"Carlie, stop."

I did not recognize the voice, I turned slowly, my hand resting on the barrel of my rifle. A young man, dressed in buckskin, and riding a spotted horse, stopped abruptly, almost running me down. In his left hand, he was holding the reins of a riderless horse. I stepped back and raised my rifle.

"Stop right there," I ordered.

He sat quietly, leaned forward in his saddle, and said nothing.

"What do you want?" I asked sharply.

"My name is Lance Johnson; Chief Johnson is my grandfather."

I stiffened and tightened my grip on my rifle. I waited for him to answer my question. After what seemed an eternity, he jumped off his horse and approached me. I warned him a second time to stop.

"My grandfather wishes me to accompany you to your destination, to make sure you arrive safely."

"I don't want anything from him or you," I spat angrily. "He's the reason I lost Taylor and Eddie, and why I had to leave Blackfoot. Get back on your horse, turn around and return to your home."

"It is not safe for a lone woman to travel through the mountains. From the way you are holding your rifle, I would say you have not used if often."

His words spoke the truth, I had no idea where I was going, I realized Little Mountain was out of the question, which left either the cabin or Princeton. I vowed I would get Eddie back, no matter what it took for me to succeed.

It was then I acknowledged I had no idea how to survive on my own, I had relied entirely on Taylor and Mai-Li during our journey and wouldn't last a day on my own. My only choice was to accept help from Lance Johnson. I lowered my rifle; walked over to the riderless horse and took the reins from Lance. I started to walk, saying nothing. Lance smiled and followed behind me.

A new chapter in my life would soon begin, I prayed I had the strength to endure what lay ahead.

The End

BWL Publishing

bwlpublishing.ca